THE MURDER
ON THE LINKS

**Center Point
Large Print**

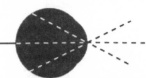

Agatha Christie

THE MURDER
ON THE LINKS

A Hercule Poirot Mystery

CENTER POINT LARGE PRINT
THORNDIKE, MAINE

This Center Point Large Print edition is published in the year 2012 by arrangement with Harper Paperbacks, an imprint of HarperCollins Publishers.

The text of this Large Print edition is unabridged. In other aspects, this book may vary from the original edition. Printed in the United States of America on permanent paper. Set in 16-point Times New Roman type.

ISBN: 978-1-61173-430-0

Library of Congress Cataloging-in-Publication Data

Christie, Agatha, 1890–1976.
The Murder on the links : a Hercule Poirot mystery / Agatha Christie.
pages ; cm.
ISBN 978-1-61173-430-0 (library binding : alk. paper)
1. Poirot, Hercule (Fictitious character)—Fiction.
2. Private investigators—England—Fiction. 3. Large type books. I. Title.
PR6005.H66M86 2012
823´.912—dc22
                                                    2012005014

To My Husband
a fellow enthusiast for detective stories
and to whom I am indebted for much
helpful advice and criticism

Contents

One

A Fellow Traveller

I believe that a well-known anecdote exists to the effect that a young writer, determined to make the commencement of his story forcible and original enough to catch and rivet the attention of the most blasé of editors, penned the following sentence:

" 'Hell!' said the Duchess."

Strangely enough, this tale of mine opens in much the same fashion. Only the lady who gave utterance to the exclamation was not a duchess.

It was a day in early June. I had been transacting some business in Paris and was returning by the morning service to London, where I was still sharing rooms with my old friend, the Belgian ex-detective, Hercule Poirot.

The Calais express was singularly empty—in fact, my own compartment held only one other traveller. I had made a somewhat hurried departure from the hotel and was busy assuring myself that I had duly collected all my traps, when the train started. Up till then I had hardly noticed my companion, but I was now violently recalled to the fact of her existence. Jumping up from her seat, she let down the window and stuck her head out, withdrawing it a moment later with the brief and forcible ejaculation "Hell!"

Now I am old-fashioned. A woman, I consider, should be womanly. I have no patience with the modern neurotic girl who jazzes from morning to night, smokes like a chimney, and uses language which would make a Billingsgate fishwoman blush!

I looked up, frowning slightly, into a pretty, impudent face, surmounted by a rakish little red hat. A thick cluster of black curls hid each ear. I judged that she was little more than seventeen, but her face was covered with powder, and her lips were quite impossibly scarlet.

Nothing abashed, she returned my glance, and executed an expressive grimace.

"Dear me, we've shocked the kind gentleman!" she observed to an imaginary audience. "I apologize for my language! Most unladylike, and all that, but, oh, Lord, there's reason enough for it! Do you know I've lost my only sister?"

"Really?" I said politely. "How unfortunate."

"He disapproves!" remarked the lady. "He disapproves utterly—of me, and my sister—which last is unfair, because he hasn't seen her!"

I opened my mouth, but she forestalled me.

"Say no more! Nobody loves me! I shall go into the garden and eat worms! Boohoo. I am crushed!"

She buried herself behind a large comic French paper. In a minute or two I saw her eyes stealthily peeping at me over the top. In spite of myself I could not help smiling, and in a minute she had tossed the paper aside, and had burst into a merry peal of laughter.

"I knew you weren't such a mutt as you looked," she cried.

Her laughter was so infectious that I could not help joining in, though I hardly cared for the word "mutt."

"There! Now we're friends!" declared the minx. "Say you're sorry about my sister—"

"I am desolated!"

"That's a good boy!"

"Let me finish. I was going to add that, although I am desolated, I can manage to put up with her absence very well." I made a little bow.

But this most unaccountable of damsels frowned and shook her head.

"Cut it out. I prefer the 'dignified disapproval' stunt. Oh, your face! 'Not one of us,' it said. And you were right there—though, mind you, it's pretty hard to tell nowadays. It's not everyone who can distinguish between a demi and a duchess. There now, I believe I've shocked you again! You've been dug out of the backwoods, you have. Not that I mind that. We could do with a few more of your sort. I just hate a fellow who gets fresh. It makes me mad."

She shook her head vigorously.

"What are you like when you're mad?" I inquired with a smile.

"A regular little devil! Don't care what I say, or what I do, either! I nearly did a chap in once. Yes, really. He'd have deserved it too."

"Well," I begged, "don't get mad with me."

"I shan't. I like you—did the first moment I set eyes on you. But you looked so disapproving that I never thought we should make friends."

"Well, we have. Tell me something about yourself."

"I'm an actress. No—not the kind you're thinking of. I've been on the boards since I was a kid of six—tumbling."

"I beg your pardon," I said, puzzled.

"Haven't you ever seen child acrobats?"

"Oh, I understand!"

"I'm American born, but I've spent most of my life in England. We've got a new show now—"

"We?"

"My sister and I. Sort of song and dance, and a bit of patter, and a dash of the old business thrown in. It's quite a new idea, and it hits them every time. There's going to be money in it—"

My new acquaintance leaned forward, and discoursed volubly, a great many of her terms being quite unintelligible to me. Yet I found myself evincing an increasing interest in her. She seemed such a curious mixture of child and woman. Though perfectly worldly-wise, and able, as she expressed it, to take care of herself, there was yet something curiously ingenuous in her

12

single-minded attitude towards life, and her wholehearted determination to "make good."

We passed through Amiens. The name awakened many memories. My companion seemed to have an intuitive knowledge of what was in my mind.

"Thinking of the War?"

I nodded.

"You were through it, I suppose?"

"Pretty well. I was wounded once, and after the Somme they invalided me out altogether. I'm a sort of private secretary now to an MP."

"My! That's brainy!"

"No, it isn't. There's really awfully little to do. Usually a couple of hours every day sees me through. It's dull work too. In fact, I don't know what I should do if I hadn't got something to fall back upon."

"Don't say you collect bugs!"

"No. I share rooms with a very interesting man. He's a Belgian—an ex-detective. He's set up as a private detective in London, and he's doing extraordinarily well. He's really a very marvellous little man. Time and again he has proved to be right where the official police have failed."

My companion listened with widening eyes.

"Isn't that interesting now? I just adore crime. I go to all the mysteries on the movies. And when there's a murder on I just devour the papers."

"Do you remember the Styles Case?" I asked.

13

"Let me see, was that the old lady who was poisoned? Somewhere down in Essex?"

I nodded.

"That was Poirot's first big case. Undoubtedly, but for him the murderer would have escaped scot-free. It was a most wonderful bit of detective work."

Warming to my subject, I ran over the heads of the affair, working up to the triumphant and unexpected dénouement.

The girl listened spellbound. In fact, we were so absorbed that the train drew into Calais station before we realized it.

I secured a couple of porters, and we alighted on the platform. My companion held out her hand.

"Goodbye, and I'll mind my language better in future."

"Oh, but surely you'll let me look after you on the boat?"

"Mayn't be on the boat. I've got to see whether that sister of mine got aboard after all anywhere. But thanks, all the same."

"Oh, but we're going to meet again, surely? Aren't you even going to tell me your name?" I cried, as she turned away.

She looked over her shoulder.

"Cinderella," she said, and laughed.

But little did I think when and how I should see Cinderella again.

Two

AN APPEAL FOR HELP

It was five minutes past nine when I entered our joint sitting room for breakfast on the following morning. My friend Poirot, exact to the minute as usual, was just tapping the shell of his second egg.

He beamed upon me as I entered.

"You have slept well, yes? You have recovered from the crossing so terrible? It is a marvel, almost you are exact this morning. *Pardon*, but your tie is not symmetrical. Permit that I rearrange him."

Elsewhere, I have described Hercule Poirot. An extraordinary little man! Height, five feet four inches, egg-shaped head carried a little to one side, eyes that shone green when he was excited, stiff military moustache, air of dignity immense! He was neat and dandified in appearance. For neatness of any kind he had an absolute passion. To see an ornament set crookedly, or a speck of dust, or a slight disarray in one's attire, was torture to the little man until he could ease his feelings by remedying the matter. "Order" and "Method" were his gods. He had a certain disdain for tangible evidence, such as footprints and cigarette ash, and would maintain that, taken by themselves, they would never enable a detective to solve a problem. Then he would tap his egg-shaped head with absurd complacency, and remark with great satisfaction: "The true work, it is done from *within*. *The little grey cells*—remember always the little grey cells, *mon ami*."

I slipped into my seat, and remarked idly, in answer to Poirot's greeting, that an hour's sea passage from Calais to Dover could hardly be dignified by the epithet "terrible."

"Anything interesting come by the post?" I asked.

Poirot shook his head with a dissatisfied air.

"I have not yet examined my letters, but nothing of interest arrives nowadays. The great criminals, the criminals of method, they do not exist."

He shook his head despondently, and I roared with laughter.

"Cheer up, Poirot, the luck will change. Open your letters. For all you know, there may be a great case looming on the horizon."

Poirot smiled, and taking up the neat little letter opener with which he opened his correspondence he slit the tops of the several envelopes that lay by his plate.

"A bill. Another bill. It is that I grow extravagant in my old age. Aha! a note from Japp."

"Yes?" I pricked up my ears. The Scotland Yard

Inspector had more than once ~~~~~~~~~
interesting case.

"He merely thanks me (in his ~~~~~~~
little point in the Aberystwyth Cas ~~~
was able to set him right. I am deligh ~~~~
been of service to him."

Poirot continued to read his correspondence placidly.

"A suggestion that I should give a lecture to our local Boy Scouts. The Countess of Forfanock will be obliged if I will call and see her. Another lapdog without doubt! And now for the last. Ah—"

I looked up, quick to notice the change of tone. Poirot was reading attentively. In a minute he tossed the sheet over to me.

"This is out of the ordinary, *mon ami*. Read for yourself."

The letter was written on a foreign type of paper, in a bold characteristic hand:

> Villa Geneviève,
> Merlinville-sur-Mer,
> France.

> Dear Sir,—I am in need of the services of a detective and, for reasons which I will give you later, do not wish to call in the official police. I have heard of you from several quarters, and all reports go to show that you are not only a man of decided

one who also knows how to be ̶ ̶ ̶ ̶eet. I do not wish to trust details to the post, but, on account of a secret I possess, I go in daily fear of my life. I am convinced that the danger is imminent, and therefore I beg that you will lose no time in crossing to France, I will send a car to meet you at Calais, if you will wire me when you are arriving. I shall be obliged if you will drop all cases you have on hand, and devote yourself solely to my interests. I am prepared to pay any compensation necessary. I shall probably need your services for a considerable period of time, as it may be necessary for you to go out to Santiago, where I spent several years of my life. I shall be content for you to name your own fee.

Assuring you once more that the matter is *urgent*.

Yours faithfully,

P. T. Renauld.

Below the signature was a hastily scrawled line, almost illegible:

"For God's sake, come!"

I handed the letter back with quickened pulses.

"At last!" I said. "Here is something distinctly out of the ordinary."

"Yes, indeed," said Poirot meditatively.

"You will go of course," I continued.

Poirot nodded. He was thinking deeply. Finally he seemed to make up his mind, and glanced up at the clock. His face was very grave.

"See you, my friend, there is no time to lose. The Continental express leaves Victoria at 11 o'clock. Do not agitate yourself. There is plenty of time. We can allow ten minutes for discussion. You accompany me, *n'est-ce pas*?"

"Well—"

"You told me yourself that your employer needed you not for the next few weeks."

"Oh, that's all right. But this Mr. Renauld hints strongly that his business is private."

"Ta-ta-ta! I will manage M. Renauld. By the way, I seem to know the name?"

"There's a well-known South American millionaire fellow. His name's Renauld. I don't know whether it could be the same."

"But without doubt. That explains the mention of Santiago. Santiago is in Chile, and Chile it is in South America! Ah; but we progress finely! You remarked the postscript? How did it strike you?"

I considered.

"Clearly he wrote the letter keeping himself well in hand, but at the end his self-control snapped and, on the impulse of the moment, he scrawled those four desperate words."

But my friend shook his head energetically.

"You are in error. See you not that while the ink of the signature is nearly black, that of the postscript is quite pale?"

"Well?" I said, puzzled.

"*Mon Dieu, mon ami*, but use your little grey cells. Is it not obvious? Mr. Renault wrote his letter. Without blotting it, he reread it carefully. Then, not on impulse, but deliberately, he added those last words, and blotted the sheet."

"But why?"

"*Parbleu*! so that it should produce the effect upon me that it has upon you."

"What?"

"*Mais oui*—to make sure of my coming! He reread the letter and was dissatisfied. It was not strong enough!"

He paused, and then added softly, his eyes shining with that green light that always betokened inward excitement:

"And so, *mon ami*, since that postscript was added, not on impulse, but soberly, in cold blood, the urgency is very great, and we must reach him as soon as possible."

"Merlinville," I murmured thoughtfully. "I've heard of it, I think."

Poirot nodded.

"It is a quiet little place—but chic! It lies about midway between Boulogne and Calais. Mr. Renauld has a house in England, I suppose?"

"Yes, in Rutland Gate, as far as I remember.

Also a big place in the country, somewhere in Hertfordshire. But I really know very little about him, he doesn't do much in a social way. I believe he has large South American interests in the City, and has spent most of his life out in Chile and the Argentine."

"Well, we shall hear all the details from the man himself. Come, let us pack. A small suitcase each, and then a taxi to Victoria."

Eleven o'clock saw our departure from Victoria on our way to Dover. Before starting Poirot had dispatched a telegram to Mr. Renauld giving the time of our arrival at Calais.

"I'm surprised you haven't invested in a few bottles of some sea sick remedy, Poirot," I observed maliciously, as I recalled our conversation at breakfast.

My friend, who was anxiously scanning the weather, turned a reproachful face upon me.

"Is it that you have forgotten the method most excellent of Laverguier? His system, I practise it always. One balances oneself, if you remember, turning the head from left to right, breathing in and out, counting six between each breath."

"H'm," I demurred. "You'll be rather tired of balancing yourself and counting six by the time you get to Santiago, or Buenos Aires, or wherever it is you land."

"*Quelle idée*! You do not figure to yourself that I shall go to Santiago?"

"Mr. Renauld suggests it in his letter."

"He did not know the methods of Hercule Poirot. I do not run to and fro, making journeys, and agitating myself. My work is done from within— *here*—" he tapped his forehead significantly.

As usual, this remark roused my argumentative faculty.

"It's all very well, Poirot, but I think you are falling into the habit of despising certain things too much. A fingerprint has led sometimes to the arrest and conviction of a murderer."

"And has, without doubt, hanged more than one innocent man," remarked Poirot dryly.

"But surely the study of fingerprints and footprints, cigarette ash, different kinds of mud, and other clues that comprise the minute observation of details—all these are of vital importance?"

"But certainly. I have never said otherwise. The trained observer, the expert, without doubt he is useful! But the others, the Hercules Poirots, they are above the experts! To them the experts bring the facts, their business is the method of the crime, its logical deduction, the proper sequence and order of the facts; above all, the true psychology of the case. You have hunted the fox, yes?"

"I have hunted a bit, now and again," I said, rather bewildered by this abrupt change of subject. "Why?"

"*Eh bien*, this hunting of the fox, you need the dogs, no?"

"Hounds," I corrected gently. "Yes, of course."

"But yet," Poirot wagged his finger at me. "You did not descend from your horse and run along the ground smelling with your nose and uttering loud Ow Ows?"

In spite of myself I laughed immoderately. Poirot nodded in a satisfied manner.

"So. You leave the work of the d— hounds to the hounds. Yet you demand that I, Hercule Poirot, should make myself ridiculous by lying down (possibly on damp grass) to study hypothetical footprints, and should scoop up cigarette ash when I do not know one kind from the other. Remember the Plymouth Express mystery. The good Japp departed to make a survey of the railway line. When he returned, I, without having moved from my apartments, was able to tell him exactly what he had found."

"So you are of the opinion that Japp wasted his time."

"Not at all, since his evidence confirmed my theory. But *I* should have wasted my time if *I* had gone. It is the same with so called 'experts.' Remember the handwriting testimony in the Cavendish Case. One counsel's questioning brings out testimony as to the resemblances, the defence brings evidence to show dissimilarity. All the language is very technical. And the result?

What we all knew in the first place. The writing was very like that of John Cavendish. And the psychological mind is faced with the question 'Why?' Because it was actually his? Or because some one wished us to think it was his? I answered that question, *mon ami*, and answered it correctly."

And Poirot, having effectually silenced, if not convinced me, leaned back with a satisfied air.

On the boat, I knew better than to disturb my friend's solitude. The weather was gorgeous, and the sea as smooth as the proverbial millpond, so I was hardly surprised when a smiling Poirot joined me on disembarking at Calais. A disappointment was in store for us, as no car had been sent to meet us, but Poirot put this down to his telegram having been delayed in transit.

"We will hire a car," he said cheerfully. And a few minutes later saw us creaking and jolting along, in the most ramshackle of automobiles that ever plied for hire, in the direction of Merlinville.

My spirits were at their highest, but my little friend was observing me gravely.

"You are what the Scotch people call 'fey,' Hastings. It presages disaster."

"Nonsense. At any rate, you do not share my feelings."

"No, but I am afraid."

"Afraid of what?"

"I do not know. But I have a premonition—a *je ne sais quoi!*"

He spoke so gravely that I was impressed in spite of myself.

"I have a feeling," he said slowly, "that this is going to be a big affair—a long, troublesome problem that will not be easy to work out."

I would have questioned him further, but we were just coming into the little town of Merlinville, and we slowed up to inquire the way to the Villa Geneviève.

"Straight on, monsieur, through the town. The Villa Geneviève is about half a mile the other side. You cannot miss it. A big villa, overlooking the sea."

We thanked our informant, and drove on, leaving the town behind. A fork in the road brought us to a second halt. A peasant was trudging towards us, and we waited for him to come up to us in order to ask the way again. There was a tiny villa standing right by the road, but it was too small and dilapidated to be the one we wanted. As we waited, the gate of it swung open and a girl came out.

The peasant was passing us now, and the driver leaned forward from his seat and asked for direction.

"The Villa Geneviève? Just a few steps up this road to the right, monsieur. You could see it if it were not for the curve."

The chauffeur thanked him, and started the car again. My eyes were fascinated by the girl who still stood, with one hand on the gate, watching us. I am an admirer of beauty, and here was one whom nobody could have passed without remark. Very tall, with the proportions of a young goddess, her uncovered golden head gleaming in the sunlight, I swore to myself that she was one of the most beautiful girls I had ever seen. As we swung up the rough road, I turned my head to look after her.

"By Jove, Poirot," I exclaimed, "did you see that young goddess?"

Poirot raised his eyebrows.

"*Ça commence!*" he murmured. "Already you have seen a goddess!"

"But, hang it all, wasn't she?"

"Possibly, I did not remark the fact."

"Surely you noticed her?"

"*Mon ami*, two people rarely see the same thing. You, for instance, saw a goddess. I—" He hesitated.

"Yes?"

"I saw only a girl with anxious eyes," said Poirot gravely.

But at that moment we drew up at a big green gate, and, simultaneously, we both uttered an exclamation. Before it stood an imposing *sergent de ville*. He held up his hand to bar our way.

"You cannot pass, messieurs."

"But we wish to see Mr. Renauld," I cried. "We have an appointment. This is his villa, isn't it?"

"Yes, monsieur, but—"

Poirot leaned forward.

"But what?"

"Monsieur Renauld was murdered this morning."

Three

AT THE VILLA GENEVIÈVE

In a moment Poirot had leapt from the car, his eyes blazing with excitement.

"What is that you say? Murdered? When? How?"

The *sergent de ville* drew himself up.

"I cannot answer any questions, monsieur."

"True. I comprehend." Poirot reflected for a minute. "The Commissary of Police, he is without doubt within?"

"Yes, monsieur."

Poirot took out a card, and scribbled a few words on it.

"*Voilà!* Will you have the goodness to see that this card is sent in to the commissary at once?"

The man took it and, turning his head over his shoulder, whistled. In a few seconds a comrade joined him, and was handed Poirot's message. There was a wait of some minutes, and then a short, stout man with a huge moustache came bustling down to the gate. The *sergent de ville* saluted and stood aside.

"My dear Monsieur Poirot," cried the new-comer, "I am delighted to see you. Your arrival is most opportune."

Poirot's face had lighted up.

"Monsieur Bex! This is indeed a pleasure." He turned to me. "This is an English friend of mine, Captain Hastings—Monsieur Lucien Bex."

The commissary and I bowed to each other ceremoniously, and M. Bex turned once more to Poirot.

"*Mon vieux*, I have not seen you since 1909, that time in Ostend. You have information to give which may assist us?"

"Possibly you know it already. You were aware that I had been sent for?"

"No. By whom?"

"The dead man. It seems that he knew an attempt was going to be made on his life. Unfortunately he sent for me too late."

"*Sacré tonnerre!*" ejaculated the Frenchman. "So he foresaw his own murder. That upsets our theories considerably! But come inside."

He held the gate open, and we commenced walking towards the house. M. Bex continued to talk:

"The examining magistrate, Monsieur Hautet, must hear of this at once. He has just finished examining the scene of the crime and is about to begin his interrogations."

"When was the crime committed?" asked Poirot.

"The body was discovered this morning about nine o'clock. Madame Renauld's evidence and that of the doctors goes to show that death must have occurred about 2 a.m. But enter, I pray of you."

We had arrived at the steps which led up to the front door of the villa. In the hall another *sergent de ville* was sitting. He rose at sight of the commissary.

"Where is Monsieur Hautet now?" inquired the latter.

"In the *salon*, monsieur."

M. Bex opened a door to the left of the hall, and we passed in. M. Hautet and his clerk were sitting at a big round table. They looked up as we entered. The commissary introduced us, and explained our presence.

M. Hautet, the Juge d'Instruction, was a tall gaunt man, with piercing dark eyes, and a neatly cut grey beard, which he had a habit of caressing as he talked. Standing by the mantelpiece was an elderly man, with slightly stooping shoulders, who was introduced to us as Dr. Durand.

"Most extraordinary," remarked M. Hautet as the commissary finished speaking. "You have the letter here, monsieur?"

Poirot handed it to him, and the magistrate read it.

"H'm! He speaks of a secret. What a pity he was not more explicit. We are much indebted to you, Monsieur Poirot. I hope you will do us the honour of assisting us in our investigations. Or are you obliged to return to London?"

"Monsieur le juge, I propose to remain. I did not arrive in time to prevent my client's death, but I feel myself bound in honour to discover the assassin."

The magistrate bowed.

"These sentiments do you honour. Also, without doubt, Madame Renauld will wish to retain your services. We are expecting M. Giraud from the Sûreté in Paris any moment, and I am sure that you and he will be able to give each other mutual assistance in your investigations. In the meantime, I hope that you will do me the honour to be present at my interrogations, and I need hardly say that if there is any assistance you require it is at your disposal."

"I thank you, monsieur. You will comprehend that at present I am completely in the dark. I know nothing whatever."

M. Hautet nodded to the commissary, and the latter took up the tale:

"This morning, the old servant Françoise, on descending to start her work, found the front door ajar. Feeling a momentary alarm as to burglars, she looked into the dining room, but seeing the silver was safe she thought no more about it, concluding that her master had, without doubt, risen early, and gone for a stroll."

"Pardon, monsieur, for interrupting, but was that a common practice of his?"

"No, it was not, but old Françoise has the common idea as regards the English—that they are mad, and liable to do the most unaccountable things at any moment! Going to call her mistress as usual, a young maid, Léonie, was horrified to discover her gagged and bound, and almost at the same moment news was brought that Monsieur Renauld's body had been discovered, stone dead, stabbed in the back."

"Where?"

"That is one of the most extraordinary features of the case. Monsieur Poirot, the body was lying face downwards, *in an open grave.*"

"What?"

"Yes. The pit was freshly dug—just a few yards outside the boundary of the villa grounds."

"And it had been dead—how long?"

Dr. Durand answered this.

"I examined the body this morning at ten o'clock. Death must have taken place at least seven, and possibly ten hours previously."

"H'm! that fixes it at between midnight and 3 a.m."

"Exactly, and Mrs. Renauld's evidence places it at after 2 a.m., which narrows the field still

31

farther. Death must have been instantaneous, and naturally could not have been self-inflicted."

Poirot nodded, and the commissary resumed:

"Madame Renauld was hastily freed from the cords that bound her by the horrified servants. She was in a terrible condition of weakness, almost unconscious from the pain of her bonds. It appears that two masked men entered the bedroom, gagged and bound her, while forcibly abducting her husband. This we know at second hand from the servants. On hearing the tragic news, she fell at once into an alarming state of agitation. On arrival, Dr. Durand immediately prescribed a sedative, and we have not yet been able to question her. But without doubt she will awake more calm, and be equal to bearing the strain of the interrogation."

The commissary paused.

"And the inmates of the house, monsieur?"

"There is old Françoise, the housekeeper, she lived for many years with the former owners of the Villa Geneviève. Then there are two young girls, sisters, Denise and Léonie Oulard. Their home is in Merlinville, and they come of most respectable parents. Then there is the chauffeur whom Monsieur Renauld brought over from England with him, but he is away on a holiday. Finally there are Madame Renauld and her son, Monsieur Jack Renauld. He, too, is away from home at present."

Poirot bowed his head. M. Hautet spoke:

"Marchaud!"

The *sergent de ville* appeared.

"Bring in the woman Françoise."

The man saluted, and disappeared. In a moment or two he returned, escorting the frightened Françoise.

"Your name is Françoise Arrichet?"

"Yes, monsieur."

"You have been a long time in service at the Villa Geneviève?"

"Eleven years with Madame la Vicomtesse. Then when she sold the Villa this spring, I consented to remain on with the English milor'. Never did I imagine—"

The magistrate cut her short.

"Without doubt, without doubt. Now, Françoise, in this matter of the front door, whose business was it to fasten it at night?"

"Mine, monsieur. Always I saw to it myself."

"And last night?"

"I fastened it as usual."

"You are sure of that?"

"I swear it by the blessed saints, monsieur."

"What time would that be?"

"The same time as usual, half past ten, monsieur."

"What about the rest of the household, had they gone up to bed?"

"Madame had retired some time before. Denise

and Léonie went up with me. Monsieur was still in his study."

"Then, if anyone unfastened the door afterwards, it must have been Monsieur Renauld himself?"

Françoise shrugged her broad shoulders.

"What should he do that for? With robbers and assassins passing every minute! A nice idea! Monsieur was not an imbecile. It is not as though he had had to let the lady out—"

The magistrate interrupted sharply:

"The lady? What lady do you mean?"

"Why, the lady who came to see him."

"Had a lady been to see him that evening?"

"But yes, monsieur—and many other evenings as well."

"Who was she? Did you know her?"

A rather cunning look spread over the woman's face.

"How should I know who it was?" she grumbled. "I did not let her in last night."

"Aha!" roared the examining magistrate, bringing his hand down with a bang on the table. "You would trifle with the police, would you? I demand that you tell me at once the name of this woman who came to visit Monsieur Renauld in the evenings."

"The police—the police," grumbled Françoise. "Never did I think that I should be mixed-up with the police. But I know well enough who she was. It was Madame Daubreuil."

The commissary uttered an exclamation, and leaned forward as though in utter astonishment.

"Madame Daubreuil—from the Villa Marguerite just down the road?"

"That is what I said, monsieur. Oh, she is a pretty one."

The old woman tossed her head scornfully.

"Madame Daubreuil," murmured the commissary. "Impossible."

"*Voilà*," grumbled Françoise. "That is all you get for telling the truth."

"Not at all," said the examining magistrate soothingly. "We were surprised, that is all. Madame Daubreuil then, and Monsieur Renauld, they were—?" He paused delicately. "Eh? It was that without doubt?"

"How should I know? But what will you? Monsieur, he was *milord anglais—très riche*—and Madame Daubreuil, she was poor, that one—and *très chic*, for all that she lives so quietly with her daughter. Not a doubt of it, she has had her history! She is no longer young, but *ma foi*! I who speak to you have seen the men's heads turn after her as she goes down the street. Besides lately, she had had more money to spend—all the town knows it. The little economies, they are at an end." And Françoise shook her head with an air of unalterable certainty.

M. Hautet stroked his beard reflectively.

"And Madame Renauld?" he asked at length. "How did she take this—friendship?"

Françoise shrugged her shoulders.

"She was always most amiable—most polite. One would say that she suspected nothing. But all the same, is it not so, the heart suffers, monsieur? Day by day, I have watched Madame grow paler and thinner. She was not the same woman who arrived here a month ago. Monsieur, too, has changed. He also has had his worries. One could see that he was on the brink of a crisis of the nerves. And who could wonder, with an affair conducted in such a fashion? No reticence, no discretion. *Style anglais*, without doubt!"

I bounded indignantly in my seat, but the examining magistrate was continuing his questions, undistracted by side issues.

"You say that Monsieur Renauld had not to let Madame Daubreuil out? Had she left, then?"

"Yes, monsieur. I heard them come out of the study and go to the door. Monsieur said goodnight, and shut the door after her."

"What time was that?"

"About twenty-five minutes after ten, monsieur."

"Do you know when Monsieur Renauld went to bed?"

"I heard him come up about ten minutes after we did. The stair creaks so that one hears everyone who goes up and down."

36

"And that is all? You heard no sound of disturbance during the night?"

"Nothing whatever, monsieur."

"Which of the servants came down the first in the morning?"

"I did, monsieur. At once I saw the door swinging open."

"What about the other downstairs windows, were they all fastened?"

"Every one of them. There was nothing suspicious or out of place anywhere."

"Good. Françoise, you can go."

The old woman shuffled towards the door. On the threshold she looked back.

"I will tell you one thing, monsieur. That Madame Daubreuil she is a bad one! Oh, yes, one woman knows about another. She is a bad one, remember that." And, shaking her head sagely, Françoise left the room.

"Léonie Oulard," called the magistrate.

Léonie appeared dissolved in tears, and inclined to be hysterical. M. Hautet dealt with her adroitly. Her evidence was mainly concerned with the discovery of her mistress gagged and bound, of which she gave rather an exaggerated account. She, like Françoise, had heard nothing during the night.

Her sister, Denise, succeeded her. She agreed that her master had changed greatly of late.

"Every day he became more and more morose.

He ate less. He was always depressed." But Denise had her own theory. "Without doubt it was the Mafia he had on his track! Two masked men— who else could it be? A terrible society that!"

"It is, of course, possible," said the magistrate smoothly. "Now, my girl, was it you who admitted Madame Daubreuil to the house last night?"

"Not *last* night, monsieur, the night before."

"But Françoise has just told us that Madame Daubreuil was here last night?"

"No, monsieur. A lady *did* come to see Monsieur Renauld last night, but it was not Madame Daubreuil."

Surprised, the magistrate insisted, but the girl held firm. She knew Madame Daubreuil perfectly by sight. This lady was dark also, but shorter, and much younger. Nothing could shake her statement.

"Had you ever seen this lady before?"

"Never, monsieur." And then the girl added diffidently: "But I think she was English."

"English?"

"Yes, monsieur. She asked for Monsieur Renauld in quite good French, but the accent— however slight one can always tell it. Besides, when they came out of the study they were speaking in English."

"Did you hear what they said? Could you understand it, I mean?"

"Me, I speak the English very well," said Denise with pride. "The lady was speaking too fast for me to catch what she said, but I heard Monsieur's last words as he opened the door for her." She paused, and then repeated carefully and laboriously: " 'Yeas—yeas—but for Gaud's saike go nauw!' "

"Yes, yes, but for God's sake go now!" repeated the magistrate.

He dismissed Denise and, after a moment or two for consideration, recalled Françoise. To her he propounded the question as to whether she had not made a mistake in fixing the night of Madame Daubreuil's visit. Françoise, however, proved unexpectedly obstinate. It was last night that Madame Daubreuil had come. Without doubt it was she. Denise wished to make herself interesting, *voilà tout*! So she had cooked up this fine tale about a strange lady. Airing her knowledge of English, too! Probably Monsieur had never spoken that sentence in English at all, and, even if he had, it proved nothing, for Madame Daubreuil spoke English perfectly, and generally used that language when talking to Monsieur and Madame Renauld. "You see, Monsieur Jack, the son of Monsieur, was usually here, and he spoke the French very badly."

The magistrate did not insist. Instead, he inquired about the chauffeur, and learned that only yesterday Monsieur Renauld had declared

39

that he was not likely to use the car, and that Masters might just as well take a holiday.

A perplexed frown was beginning to gather between Poirot's eyes.

"What is it?" I whispered.

He shook his head impatiently, and asked a question:

"Pardon, Monsieur Bex, but without doubt Monsieur Renauld could drive the car himself?"

The commissary looked over at Françoise, and the old woman replied promptly:

"No, Monsieur did not drive himself."

Poirot's frown deepened.

"I wish you would tell me what is worrying you," I said impatiently.

"See you not? In his letter Monsieur Renauld speaks of sending the car for me to Calais."

"Perhaps he meant a hired car," I suggested.

"Doubtless, that is so. But why hire a car when you have one of your own? Why choose yesterday to send away the chauffeur on a holiday—suddenly, at a moment's notice? Was it that for some reason he wanted him out of the way before we arrived?"

Four

THE LETTER SIGNED "BELLA"

Françoise had left the room. The magistrate was drumming thoughtfully on the table.

"Monsieur Bex," he said at length, "here we have directly conflicting testimony. Which are we to believe, Françoise or Denise?"

"Denise," said the commissary decidedly. "It was she who let the visitor in. Françoise is old and obstinate, and has evidently taken a dislike to Madame Daubreuil. Besides, our own knowledge tends to show that Renauld was entangled with another woman."

"*Tiens!*" cried M. Hautet. "We have forgotten to inform Monsieur Poirot of that." He searched among the papers on the table, and finally handed the one he was in search of to my friend. "This letter, Monsieur Poirot, we found in the pocket of the dead man's overcoat."

Poirot took it and unfolded it. It was somewhat worn and crumpled, and was written in English in a rather unformed hand:

My Dearest One,—Why have you not written for so long? You do love me still, don't you? Your letters lately have been so different, cold, and strange, and now this long silence. It makes me afraid. If you were to stop loving me! But that's impossible—what a silly kid I am—always imagining things! But if you *did* stop loving me, I don't know what I should do—kill myself perhaps! I couldn't live without you. Sometimes I fancy another woman is coming between us. Let her look out, that's all—and you too! I'd as soon kill you as let her have you! I mean it.

But there, I'm writing high-flown nonsense. You love me, and I love you— yes, love you, love you, love you!

Your own adoring

Bella.

There was no address or date. Poirot handed it back with a grave face.

"And the assumption is—?"

The examining magistrate shrugged his shoulders.

"Obviously Monsieur Renauld was entangled with this Englishwoman—Bella! He comes over here, meets Madame Daubreuil, and starts an intrigue with her. He cools off to the other, and she instantly suspects something. This letter contains a distinct threat. Monsieur Poirot, at first sight the case seemed simplicity itself. Jealousy! The fact that Monsieur Renauld was stabbed in

42

the back seemed to point distinctly to its being a woman's crime."

Poirot nodded.

"The stab in the back, yes—but not the grave! That was laborious work, hard work—no woman dug that grave, Monsieur. That was a man's doing."

The commissary exclaimed excitedly:

"Yes, yes, you are right. We did not think of that."

"As I said," continued M. Hautet, "at first sight the case seemed simple, but the masked men, and the letter you received from Monsieur Renauld, complicate matters. Here we seem to have an entirely different set of circumstances, with no relationship between the two. As regards the letter written to yourself, do you think it is possible that it referred in any way to this 'Bella' and her threats?"

Poirot shook his head.

"Hardly. A man like Monsieur Renauld, who had led an adventurous life in out-of-the-way places, would not be likely to ask for protection against a woman."

The examining magistrate nodded his head emphatically.

"My view exactly. Then we must look for the explanation of the letter—"

"In Santiago," finished the commissary. "I shall cable without delay to the police in that city, requesting full details of the murdered man's life out there, his love affairs, his business transactions, his friendships, and any enmities he may have incurred. It will be strange if, after that, we do not hold a clue to his mysterious murder."

The commissary looked around for approval.

"Excellent!" said Poirot appreciatively.

"You have found no other letters from this Bella among Monsieur Renauld's effects?" asked Poirot.

"No. Of course one of our first proceedings was to search through his private papers in the study. We found nothing of interest, however. All seemed square and aboveboard. The only thing at all out of the ordinary was his will. Here it is."

Poirot ran through the document.

"So. A legacy of a thousand pounds to Mr. Stonor—who is he, by the way?"

"Monsieur Renauld's secretary. He remained in England, but was over here once or twice for a weekend."

"And everything else left unconditionally to his beloved wife, Eloise. Simply drawn up, but perfectly legal. Witnessed by the two servants, Denise and Françoise. Nothing so very unusual about that." He handed it back.

"Perhaps," began Bex, "you did not notice—"

"The date?" twinkled Poirot. "But, yes, I noticed it. A fortnight ago. Possibly it marks his first intimation of danger. Many rich men die intestate through never considering the likelihood of their demise. But it is dangerous to draw conclusions prematurely. It points, however, to his having a real liking and fondness for his wife, in spite of his amorous intrigues."

"Yes," said M. Hautet doubtfully. "But it is possibly a little unfair on his son, since it leaves him entirely dependent on his mother. If she were to marry again, and her second husband obtained an ascendancy over her, this boy might never touch a penny of his father's money."

Poirot shrugged his shoulders.

"Man is a vain animal. Monsieur Renauld figured to himself, without doubt, that his widow would never marry again. As to the son, it may have been a wise precaution to leave the money in his mother's hands. The sons of rich men are proverbially wild."

"It may be as you say. Now, Monsieur Poirot, you would without doubt like to visit the scene of the crime. I am sorry that the body has been removed, but of course photographs have been taken from every conceivable angle, and will be at your disposal as soon as they are available."

"I thank you, monsieur, for all your courtesy."

The commissary rose.

"Come with me, messieurs."

He opened the door, and bowed ceremoniously to Poirot to precede him. Poirot, with equal

45

politeness, drew back and bowed to the commissary.

"Monsieur."

"Monsieur."

At last they got out into the hall.

"That room there, it is the study, *hein*?" asked Poirot suddenly, nodding towards the door opposite.

"Yes. You would like to see it?" He threw open the door as he spoke, and we entered.

The room which M. Renauld had chosen for his own particular use was small, but furnished with great taste and comfort. A businesslike writing desk, with many pigeonholes, stood in the window. Two large leather-covered armchairs faced the fireplace, and between them was a round table covered with the latest books and magazines.

Poirot stood a moment taking in the room, then he stepped forward, passed his hand lightly over the backs of the leather chairs, picked up a magazine from the table, and drew a finger gingerly over the surface of the oak sideboard. His face expressed complete approval.

"No dust?" I asked, with a smile.

He beamed on me, appreciative of my knowledge of his peculiarities.

"Not a particle, *mon ami*! And for once, perhaps, it is a pity."

His sharp, birdlike eyes darted here and there.

"Ah!" he remarked suddenly, with an intonation of relief. "The hearthrug is crooked," and he bent down to straighten it.

Suddenly he uttered an exclamation and rose. In his hand he held a small fragment of pink paper.

"In France, as in England," he remarked, "the domestics omit to sweep under the mats?"

Bex took the fragment from him, and I came close to examine it.

"You recognize it—eh, Hastings?"

I shook my head, puzzled—and yet that particular shade of pink paper was very familiar.

The commissary's mental processes were quicker than mine.

"A fragment of a cheque," he exclaimed.

The piece of paper was roughly about two inches square. On it was written in ink the word "Duveen."

"*Bien!*" said Bex. "This cheque was payable to, or drawn by, someone named Duveen."

"The former, I fancy," said Poirot. "For, if I am not mistaken, the handwriting is that of Monsieur Renauld."

That was soon established, by comparing it with a memorandum from the desk.

"Dear me," murmured the commissary, with a crestfallen air, "I really cannot imagine how I came to overlook this."

Poirot laughed.

"The moral of that is, always look under the

mats! My friend Hastings here will tell you that anything in the least crooked is a torment to me. As soon as I saw that the hearthrug was out of the straight, I said to myself: '*Tiens*! The legs of the chair caught it in being pushed back. Possibly there may be something beneath it which the good Françoise overlooked.'"

"Françoise?"

"Or Denise, or Léonie. Whoever did this room. Since there is no dust, the room *must* have been done this morning. I reconstruct the incident like this. Yesterday, possibly last night, Monsieur Renauld drew a cheque to the order of some one named Duveen. Afterwards it was torn up, and scattered on the floor. This morning—"

But M. Bex was already pulling impatiently at the bell.

Françoise answered it. Yes, there had been a lot of pieces of paper on the floor. What had she done with them? Put them in the kitchen stove of course! What else?

With a gesture of despair, Bex dismissed her. Then, his face lightening, he ran to the desk. In a minute he was hunting through the dead man's cheque book. Then he repeated his former gesture. The last counterfoil was blank.

"Courage!" cried Poirot, clapping him on the back. "Without doubt, Madame Renauld will be able to tell us all about this mysterious person named Duveen."

The commissary's face cleared. "That is true. Let us proceed."

As we turned to leave the room, Poirot remarked casually: "It was here that Monsieur Renauld received his guest last night, eh?"

"It was—but how did you know?"

"By *this*. I found it on the back of the leather chair." And he held up between his finger and thumb a long black hair—a woman's hair!

M. Bex took us out by the back of the house to where there was a small shed leaning against the house. He produced a key from his pocket and unlocked it.

"The body is here. We moved it from the scene of the crime just before you arrived, as the photographers had done with it."

He opened the door and we passed in. The murdered man lay on the ground, with a sheet over him. M. Bex dexterously whipped off the covering. Renauld was a man of medium height, slender, and lithe in figure. He looked about fifty years of age, and his dark hair was plentifully streaked with grey. He was clean-shaven with a long, thin nose, and eyes set rather close together, and his skin was deeply bronzed, as that of a man who had spent most of his life beneath tropical skies. His lips were drawn back from his teeth and an expression of absolute amazement and terror was stamped on the livid features.

"One can see by his face that he was stabbed in the back," remarked Poirot.

Very gently, he turned the dead man over. There, between the shoulder blades, staining the light fawn overcoat, was a round dark patch. In the middle of it there was a slit in the cloth. Poirot examined it narrowly.

"Have you any idea with what weapon the crime was committed?"

"It was left in the wound." The commissary reached down a large glass jar. In it was a small object that looked to me more like a paper knife than anything else. It had a black handle and a narrow shining blade. The whole thing was not more than ten inches long. Poirot tested the discoloured point gingerly with his fingertip.

"*Ma foi*! but it is sharp! A nice easy little tool for murder!"

"Unfortunately, we could find no trace of fingerprints on it," remarked Bex regretfully. "The murderer must have worn gloves."

"Of course he did," said Poirot contemptuously. "Even in Santiago they know enough for that. The veriest amateur of an English Mees knows it—thanks to the publicity the Bertillon system has been given in the Press. All the same, it interests me very much that there were no fingerprints. It is so amazingly simple to leave the fingerprints of someone else! And then the police are happy." He shook his head. "I very much fear our criminal is not a man of method—either that or he was pressed for time. But we shall see."

He let the body fall back into its original position.

"He wore only underclothes under his overcoat, I see," he remarked.

"Yes, the examining magistrate thinks that is rather a curious point."

At this minute there was a tap on the door which Bex had closed after him. He strode forward and opened it. Françoise was there. She endeavoured to peep in with ghoulish curiosity.

"Well, what is it?" demanded Bex impatiently.

"Madame. She sends a message that she is much recovered and is quite ready to receive the examining magistrate."

"Good," said M. Bex briskly. "Tell Monsieur Hautet and say that we will come at once."

Poirot lingered a moment, looking back towards the body. I thought for a moment that he was going to apostrophize it, to declare aloud his determination never to rest till he had discovered the murderer. But when he spoke, it was tamely and awkwardly, and his comment was ludicrously inappropriate to the solemnity of the moment.

"He wore his overcoat very long," he said constrainedly.

Five

MRS. RENAULD'S STORY

We found M. Hautet awaiting us in the hall, and we all proceeded upstairs together, Françoise marching ahead to show us the way. Poirot went up in a zigzag fashion which puzzled me, until he whispered with a grimace:

"No wonder the servants heard M. Renauld mounting the stairs, not a board of them but creaks fit to awake the dead!"

At the head of the staircase, a small passage branched off.

"The servants' quarters," explained Bex.

We continued along a corridor, and Françoise tapped on the last door to the right of it.

A faint voice bade us enter, and we passed into a large, sunny apartment looking out towards the sea, which showed blue and sparkling about a quarter of a mile distant.

On a couch, propped up with cushions, and attended by Dr. Durand, lay a tall, striking-looking woman. She was middle-aged, and her once dark hair was now almost entirely silvered, but the intense vitality, and strength of her personality would have made itself felt anywhere. You knew at once that you were in the presence of what the French call *une maîtresse femme*.

She greeted us with a dignified inclination of the head.

"Pray be seated, messieurs."

We took chairs, and the magistrate's clerk established himself at a round table.

"I hope, madame," began M. Hautet, "that it will not distress you unduly to relate to us what occurred last night?"

"Not at all, monsieur. I know the value of time, if these scoundrelly assassins are to be caught and punished."

"Very well, madame. It will fatigue you less, I think, if I ask you questions and you confine yourself to answering them. At what time did you go to bed last night?"

"At half past nine, monsieur. I was tired."

"And your husband?"

"About an hour later, I fancy."

"Did he seem disturbed—upset in any way?"

"No, not more than usual."

"What happened then?"

"We slept. I was awakened by a hand pressed over my mouth. I tried to scream out, but the hand prevented me. There were two men in the room. They were both masked."

"Can you describe them at all, madame?"

"One was very tall, and had a long black beard, the other was short and stout. His beard was reddish. They both wore hats pulled down over their eyes."

"H'm!" said the magistrate thoughtfully. "Too much beard, I fear."

"You mean they were false?"

"Yes, madame. But continue your story."

"It was the short man who was holding me. He forced a gag into my mouth, and then bound me with rope hand and foot. The other man was standing over my husband. He had caught up my little dagger paper knife from the dressing table and was holding it with the point just over his heart. When the short man had finished with me, he joined the other, and they forced my husband to get up and accompany them into the dressing room next door. I was nearly fainting with terror, nevertheless I listened desperately.

"They were speaking in too low a tone for me to hear what they said. But I recognized the language, a bastard Spanish such as is spoken in some parts of South America. They seemed to be demanding something from my husband, and presently they grew angry, and their voices rose a little. I think the tall man was speaking. 'You know what we want?' he said. '*The secret!* Where is it?' I do not know what my husband answered, but the other replied fiercely: 'You lie! We know you have it. Where are your keys?'

"Then I heard sounds of drawers being pulled out. There is a safe on the wall of my husband's dressing room in which he always keeps a fairly

54

large amount of ready money. Léonie tells me this has been rifled and the money taken, but evidently what they were looking for was not there, for presently I heard the tall man, with an oath, command my husband to dress himself. Soon after that, I think some noise in the house must have disturbed them, for they hustled my husband out into my room only half-dressed."

"*Pardon*," interrupted Poirot, "but is there then no other egress from the dressing room?"

"No, monsieur, there is only the communicating door into my room. They hurried my husband through, the short man in front, and the tall man behind him with the dagger still in his hand. Paul tried to break away to come to me. I saw his agonized eyes. He turned to his captors. 'I must speak to her,' he said. Then, coming to the side of the bed, 'It is all right, Eloise,' he said. 'Do not be afraid. I shall return before morning.' But, although he tried to make his voice confident, I could see the terror in his eyes. Then they hustled him out of the door, the tall man saying: 'One sound—and you are a dead man, remember.'

"After that," continued Mrs. Renauld, "I must have fainted. The next thing I recollect is Léonie rubbing my wrists and giving me brandy."

"Madame Renauld," said the magistrate, "had you any idea what it was for which the assassins were searching?"

"None whatever, monsieur."

"Had you any knowledge that your husband feared something?"

"Yes. I had seen the change in him."

"How long ago was that?"

Mrs. Renauld reflected.

"Ten days, perhaps."

"Not longer?"

"Possibly. I only noticed it then."

"Did you question your husband at all as to the cause?"

"Once. He put me off evasively. Nevertheless, I was convinced that he was suffering some terrible anxiety. However, since he evidently wished to conceal the fact from me, I tried to pretend that I had noticed nothing."

"Were you aware that he had called in the services of a detective?"

"A detective?" exclaimed Mrs. Renauld, very much surprised.

"Yes, this gentleman—Monsieur Hercule Poirot." Poirot bowed. "He arrived today in response to a summons from your husband." And taking the letter written by M. Renauld from his pocket he handed it to the lady.

She read it with apparently genuine astonishment.

"I had no idea of this. Evidently he was fully cognizant of the danger."

"Now, madame, I will beg of you to be frank with me. Is there any incident in your husband's past life in South America which might throw light on his murder?"

Mrs. Renauld reflected deeply, but at last shook her head.

"I can think of none. Certainly my husband had many enemies, people he had got the better of in some way or another, but I can think of no one distinctive case. I do not say there is no such incident—only that I am not aware of it."

The examining magistrate stroked his beard disconsolately.

"And you can fix the time of this outrage?"

"Yes, I distinctly remember hearing the clock on the mantelpiece strike two." She nodded towards an eight-day travelling clock in a leather case which stood in the centre of the chimney-piece.

Poirot rose from his seat, scrutinized the clock carefully, and nodded, satisfied.

"And here too," exclaimed M. Bex, "is a wristwatch, knocked off the dressing table by the assassins, without doubt, and smashed to atoms. Little did they know it would testify against them."

Gently he picked away the fragments of broken glass. Suddenly his face changed to one of utter stupefaction.

"*Mon Dieu!*" he ejaculated.

"What is it?"

"The hands of the watch point to seven o'clock!"

"What?" cried the examining magistrate, astonished.

But Poirot, deft as ever, took the broken trinket from the startled commissary, and held it to his ear. Then he smiled.

"The glass is broken, yes, but the watch itself is still going."

The explanation of the mystery was greeted with a relieved smile. But the magistrate bethought him of another point.

"But surely it is not seven o'clock now?"

"No," said Poirot gently, "it is a few minutes after five. Possibly the watch gains, is that so, madame?"

Mrs. Renauld was frowning perplexedly.

"It does gain," she admitted. "But I've never known it gain quite so much as that."

With a gesture of impatience the magistrate left the matter of the watch and proceeded with his interrogatory.

"Madame, the front door was found ajar. It seems almost certain that the murderers entered that way, yet it has not been forced at all. Can you suggest any explanation?"

"Possibly my husband went out for a stroll the last thing, and forgot to latch it when he came in."

"Is that a likely thing to happen?"

"Very. My husband was the most absentminded of men."

There was a slight frown on her brow as she

spoke, as though this trait in the dead man's character had at times vexed her.

"There is one inference I think we might draw," remarked the commissary suddenly. "Since the men insisted on Monsieur Renauld dressing himself, it looks as though the place they were taking him to, the place where 'the secret' was concealed, lay some distance away."

The magistrate nodded.

"Yes, far, and yet not too far, since he spoke of being back by morning."

"What time does the last train leave the station of Merlinville?" asked Poirot.

"11:50 one way, and 12:17 the other, but it is more probable that they had a motor waiting."

"Of course," agreed Poirot, looking somewhat crestfallen.

"Indeed, that might be one way of tracing them," continued the magistrate, brightening. "A motor containing two foreigners is quite likely to have been noticed. That is an excellent point, Monsieur Bex."

He smiled to himself, and then, becoming grave once more, he said to Mrs. Renauld:

"There is another question. Do you know anyone of the name of 'Duveen'?"

"Duveen?" Mrs. Renauld repeated thoughtfully. "No, for the moment, I cannot say I do."

"You have never heard your husband mention anyone of that name."

"Never."

"Do you know anyone whose Christian name is Bella?"

He watched Mrs. Renauld narrowly as he spoke, seeking to surprise any signs of anger or consciousness, but she merely shook her head in quite a natural manner. He continued his questions.

"Are you aware that your husband had a visitor last night?"

Now he saw the red mount slightly in her cheeks, but she replied composedly:

"No, who was that?"

"A lady."

"Indeed?"

But for the moment the magistrate was content to say no more. It seemed unlikely that Madame Daubreuil had any connexion with the crime, and he was anxious not to upset Mrs. Renauld more than necessary.

He made a sign to the commissary, and the latter replied with a nod. Then rising, he went across the room, and returned with the glass jar we had seen in the outhouse in his hand. From this he took the dagger.

"Madame," he said gently, "do you recognize this?"

She gave a little cry.

"Yes, that is my little dagger." Then she saw the stained point, and she drew back, her eyes widening with horror. "Is that—blood?"

"Yes, madame. Your husband was killed with this weapon." He removed it hastily from sight. "You are quite sure about its being the one that was on your dressing table last night?"

"Oh, yes. It was a present from my son. He was in the Air Force during the War. He gave his age as older than it was." There was a touch of the proud mother in her voice. "This was made from a streamline aeroplane wire, and was given to me by my son as a souvenir of the War."

"I see, madame. That brings us to another matter. Your son, where is he now? It is necessary that he should be telegraphed to without delay."

"Jack? He is on his way to Buenos Aires."

"What?"

"Yes. My husband telegraphed to him yesterday. He had sent him on business to Paris, but yesterday he discovered that it would be necessary for him to proceed without delay to South America. There was a boat leaving Cherbourg for Buenos Aires last night, and he wired him to catch it."

"Have you any knowledge of what the business in Buenos Aires was?"

"No, monsieur, I know nothing of its nature, but Buenos Aires is not my son's final destination. He was going overland from there to Santiago."

And, in unison, the magistrate and the commissary exclaimed:

"Santiago! Again Santiago!"

It was at this moment, when we were all stunned by the mention of that word, that Poirot approached Mrs. Renauld. He had been standing by the window like a man lost in a dream, and I doubt if he had fully taken in what had passed. He paused by the lady's side with a bow.

"*Pardon*, madame, but may I examine your wrists?"

Though slightly surprised at the request, Mrs. Renauld held them out to him. Round each of them was a cruel red mark where the cords had bitten into the flesh. As he examined them, I fancied that a momentary flicker of excitement I had seen in his eyes disappeared.

"They must cause you great pain," he said, and once more he looked puzzled.

But the magistrate was speaking excitedly.

"Young Monsieur Renauld must be communicated with at once by wireless. It is vital that we should know anything he can tell us about this trip to Santiago." He hesitated. "I hoped he might have been near at hand, so that we could have saved you pain, madame." He paused.

"You mean," she said in a low voice, "the identification of my husband's body?"

The magistrate bowed his head.

"I am a strong woman, monsieur. I can bear all that is required of me. I am ready—now."

"Oh, tomorrow will be quite soon enough, I assure you—"

"I prefer to get it over," she said in a low tone, a spasm of pain crossing her face. "If you will be so good as to give me your arm, doctor?"

The doctor hastened forward, a cloak was thrown over Mrs. Renauld's shoulders, and a slow procession went down the stairs. M. Bex hurried on ahead to open the door of the shed. In a minute or two Mrs. Renauld appeared in the doorway. She was very pale, but resolute. She raised her hand to her face.

"A moment, messieurs, while I steel myself."

She took her hand away and looked down at the dead man. Then the marvellous self-control which had upheld her so far deserted her.

"Paul!" she cried. "Husband! Oh, God!" And pitching forward she fell unconscious to the ground.

Instantly Poirot was beside her, he raised the lid of her eye, felt her pulse. When he had satisfied himself that she had really fainted, he drew aside. He caught me by the arm.

"I am an imbecile, my friend! If ever there was love and grief in a woman's voice, I heard it then. My little idea was all wrong. *Eh bien*! I must start again!"

Six

THE SCENE OF THE CRIME

Between them, the doctor and M. Hautet carried the unconscious woman into the house. The commissary looked after them, shaking his head.

"*Pauvre femme*," he murmured to himself. "The shock was too much for her. Well, well, we can do nothing. Now, Monsieur Poirot, shall we visit the place where the crime was committed?"

"If you please, Monsieur Bex."

We passed through the house, and out by the front door. Poirot had looked up at the staircase in passing, and shook his head in a dissatisfied manner.

"It is to me incredible that the servants heard nothing. The creaking of that staircase, with *three* people descending it, would awaken the dead!"

"It was the middle of the night, remember. They were sound asleep by then."

But Poirot continued to shake his head as though not fully accepting the explanation. On the sweep of the drive he paused, looking up at the house.

"What moved them in the first place to try if the front door were open? It was a most unlikely thing that it should be. It was far more probable that they should at once try to force a window."

"But all the windows on the ground floor are barred with iron shutters," objected the commissary.

Poirot pointed to a window on the first floor.

"That is the window of the bedroom we have just come from, is it not? And see—there is a tree by which it would be the easiest thing in the world to mount."

"Possibly," admitted the other. "But they could not have done so without leaving footprints in the flower bed."

I saw the justice of his words. There were two large oval flower beds planted with scarlet geraniums, one each side of the steps leading up to the front door. The tree in question had its roots actually at the back of the bed itself, and it would have been impossible to reach it without stepping on the bed.

"You see," continued the commissary, "owing to the dry weather no prints would show on the drive or paths; but, on the soft mould of the flower bed, it would have been a very different affair."

Poirot went close to the bed and studied it attentively. As Bex had said, the mould was perfectly smooth. There was not an indentation on it anywhere.

Poirot nodded, as though convinced, and we turned away, but he suddenly darted off and began examining the other flower bed.

"Monsieur Bex!" he called. "See here. Here are plenty of traces for you."

The commissary joined him—and smiled.

"My dear Monsieur Poirot, those are without doubt the footprints of the gardener's large hobnailed boots. In any case, it would have no importance, since this side we have no tree, and consequently no means of gaining access to the upper storey."

"True," said Poirot, evidently crestfallen. "So you think these footprints are of no importance?"

"Not the least in the world."

Then, to my utter astonishment, Poirot pronounced these words:

"I do not agree with you. I have a little idea that these footprints are the most important things we have seen yet."

M. Bex said nothing, merely shrugged his shoulders. He was far too courteous to utter his real opinion.

"Shall we proceed?" he asked, instead.

"Certainly. I can investigate this matter of the footprints later," said Poirot cheerfully.

Instead of following the drive down to the gate, M. Bex turned up a path that branched off at right angles. It led, up a slight incline, round to the right of the house, and was bordered on either side by a kind of shrubbery. Suddenly it emerged into a little clearing from which one obtained a view of the sea. A seat had been placed here, and not far from it was a rather ramshackle shed. A few steps farther on, a neat line of small bushes marked the boundary of the Villa grounds. M. Bex pushed his way through these, and we found ourselves on a wide stretch of open downs. I looked round, and saw something that filled me with astonishment.

"Why, this is a Golf Course," I cried.

Bex nodded.

"The links are not completed yet," he explained. "It is hoped to be able to open them some time next month. It was some of the men working on them who discovered the body early this morning."

I gave a gasp. A little to my left, where for the moment I had overlooked it, was a long narrow pit and by it, face downwards, was the body of a man! For a moment my heart gave a terrible leap, and I had a wild fancy that the tragedy had been duplicated. But the commissary dispelled my illusion by moving forward with a sharp exclamation of annoyance:

"What have my police been about? They had strict orders to allow no one near the place without proper credentials!"

The man on the ground turned his head over his shoulder.

"But I have proper credentials," he remarked, and rose slowly to his feet.

"My dear Monsieur Giraud," cried the

67

commissary. "I had no idea that you had arrived, even. The examining magistrate has been awaiting you with the utmost impatience."

As he spoke, I was scanning the newcomer with the keenest curiosity. The famous detective from the Paris Sûreté was familiar to me by name, and I was extremely interested to see him in the flesh. He was very tall, perhaps about thirty years of age, with auburn hair and moustache, and a military carriage. There was a trace of arrogance in his manner which showed that he was fully alive to his own importance. Bex introduced us, presenting Poirot as a colleague. A flicker of interest came into the detective's eye.

"I know you by name, Monsieur Poirot," he said. "You cut quite a figure in the old days, didn't you? But methods are very different now."

"Crimes, though, are very much the same," remarked Poirot gently.

I saw at once that Giraud was prepared to be hostile. He resented the other being associated with him, and I felt that if he came across any clue of importance he would be more than likely to keep it to himself.

"The examining magistrate—" began Bex again.

But Giraud interrupted rudely:

"A fig for the examining magistrate! The light is the important thing. For all practical purposes it will be gone in another half hour or so. I know all about the case, and the people at the house will do very well until tomorrow; but, if we're going to find a clue to the murderers, here is the spot we shall find it. Is it your police who have been trampling all over the place? I thought they knew better nowadays."

"Assuredly they do. The marks you complain of were made by the workmen who discovered the body."

The other grunted disgustedly.

"I can see the tracks where the three of them came through the hedge—but they were cunning. You can just recognize the centre footmarks as those of Monsieur Renauld, but those on either side have been carefully obliterated. Not that there would really be much to see anyway on this hard ground, but they weren't taking any chances."

"The external sign," said Poirot. "That is what you seek, eh?"

The other detective stared.

"Of course."

A very faint smile came to Poirot's lips. He seemed about to speak, but checked himself. He bent down to where a spade was lying.

"That's what the grave was dug with, right enough," said Giraud. "But you'll get nothing from it. It was Renauld's own spade, and the man who used it wore gloves. Here they are." He gesticulated with his foot to where two soil-stained gloves were lying. "And they're Renauld's too—or at least his gardener's. I tell you, the men who carried out this crime were taking no chances. The man was stabbed with his own dagger, and would have been buried with his own spade. They counted on leaving no traces! But I'll beat them. There's always *something!* And I mean to find it."

But Poirot was now apparently interested in something else, a short, discoloured piece of lead-piping which lay beside the spade. He touched it delicately with his finger.

"And does this, too, belong to the murdered man?" he asked, and I thought I detected a subtle flavour of irony in the question.

Giraud shrugged his shoulders to indicate that he neither knew nor cared.

"May have been lying around here for weeks. Anyway, it doesn't interest me."

"I, on the contrary, find it very interesting," said Poirot sweetly.

I guessed that he was merely bent on annoying the Paris detective and, if so, he succeeded. The other turned away rudely, remarking that he had no time to waste, and bending down he resumed his minute search of the ground.

Meanwhile, Poirot, as though struck by a sudden idea, stepped back over the boundary, and tried the door of the little shed.

"That's locked," said Giraud over his shoulder.

"But it's only a place where the gardener keeps his rubbish. The spade didn't come from there, but from the toolshed up by the house."

"Marvellous," murmured M. Bex ecstatically to me. "He has been here but half an hour, and he already knows everything! What a man! Undoubtedly Giraud is the greatest detective alive today."

Although I disliked the detective heartily, I nevertheless was secretly impressed. Efficiency seemed to radiate from the man. I could not help feeling that, so far, Poirot had not greatly distinguished himself, and it vexed me. He seemed to be directing his attention to all sorts of silly puerile points that had nothing to do with the case. Indeed, at this juncture, he suddenly asked:

"Monsieur Bex, tell me, I pray you, the meaning of this whitewashed line that extends all round the grave. Is it a device of the police?"

"No, Monsieur Poirot, it is an affair of the golf course. It shows that there is here to be a 'bunkair,' as you call it."

"A bunkair?" Poirot turned to me. "That is the irregular hole filled with sand and a bank at one side, is it not?"

I concurred.

"Monsieur Renauld, without doubt he played the golf?"

"Yes, he was a keen golfer. It's mainly owing to him, and to his large subscriptions, that this work is being carried forward. He even had a say in the designing of it."

Poirot nodded thoughtfully. Then he remarked:

"It was not a very good choice they made—of a spot to bury the body? When the men began to dig up the ground, all would have been discovered."

"Exactly," cried Giraud triumphantly. "And that *proves* that they were strangers to the place. It's an excellent piece of indirect evidence."

"Yes," said Poirot doubtfully. "No one who knew would bury a body there—unless they *wanted* it to be discovered. And that is clearly absurd, is it not?"

Giraud did not even trouble to reply.

"Yes," said Poirot, in a somewhat dissatisfied voice. "Yes—undoubtedly—absurd!"

Seven

THE MYSTERIOUS MADAME DAUBREUIL

As we retraced our steps to the house, M. Bex excused himself for leaving us, explaining that he must immediately acquaint the examining magistrate with the fact of Giraud's arrival. Giraud himself had been obviously delighted when Poirot declared that he had seen all he wanted. The last thing we observed, as we left the spot, was Giraud, crawling about on all fours, with a thoroughness in his search that I could not but admire. Poirot guessed my thoughts, for as soon as we were alone he remarked ironically:

"At last you have seen the detective you admire—the human foxhound! Is it not so, my friend?"

"At any rate, he's *doing* something," I said, with asperity. "If there's anything to find he'll find it. Now you—"

"*Eh bien*! I also have found something! A piece of lead-piping."

"Nonsense, Poirot. You know very well that's got nothing to do with it. I meant *little* things—traces that may lead us infallibly to the murderers."

"*Mon ami*, a clue of two feet long is every bit as valuable as one measuring two millimetres! But it is the romantic idea that all important clues must be infinitesimal. As to the piece of lead-piping having nothing to do with the crime, you say that because Giraud told you so. No"—as I was about to interpose a question—"we will say no more. Leave Giraud to his search, and me to my ideas. The case seems straightforward enough—and yet—and yet, *mon ami*, I am not satisfied! And do you know why? Because of the wristwatch that is two hours fast. And then there are several curious little points that do not seem to fit in. For instance, if the object of the murderers was

73

revenge, why did they not stab Renauld in his sleep and have done with it?"

"They wanted the 'secret,'" I reminded him.

Poirot brushed a speck of dust from his sleeve with a dissatisfied air.

"Well, where is this 'secret'? Presumably some distance away, since they wish him to dress himself. Yet he is found murdered close at hand, almost within earshot of the house. Then again, it is pure chance that a weapon such as the dagger should be lying about casually, ready to hand."

He paused, frowning, and then went on:

"Why did the servants hear nothing? Were they drugged? Was there an accomplice, and did that accomplice see to it that the front door should remain open? I wonder if—"

He stopped abruptly. We had reached the drive in front of the house. Suddenly he turned to me.

"My friend, I am about to surprise you—to please you! I have taken your reproaches to heart! We will examine some footprints!"

"Where?"

"In that right-hand bed yonder. Monsieur Bex says that they are the footmarks of the gardener. Let us see if this is so. See, he approaches with his wheelbarrow."

Indeed an elderly man was just crossing the drive with a barrowful of seedlings. Poirot called to him, and he set down the barrow and came hobbling towards us.

"You are going to ask him for one of his boots to compare with the footmarks?" I asked breathlessly. My faith in Poirot revived a little. Since he said the footprints in this right-hand bed were important, presumably they *were*.

"Exactly," said Poirot.

"But won't he think it very odd?"

"He will not think about it at all."

We could say no more, for the old man had joined us.

"You want me for something, monsieur?"

"Yes. You have been gardener here a long time, haven't you?"

"Twenty-four years, monsieur."

"And your name is—?"

"Auguste, monsieur."

"I was admiring these magnificent geraniums. They are truly superb. They have been planted long?"

"Some time, monsieur. But of course, to keep the beds looking smart, one must keep bedding out a few new plants, and remove those that are over, besides keeping the old blooms well picked off."

"You put in some new plants yesterday, didn't you? Those in the middle there, and in the other bed also."

"Monsieur has a sharp eye. It takes always a day or so for them to 'pick up.' Yes, I put ten new plants in each bed last night. As monsieur doubtless knows, one should not put in plants when the sun is hot." Auguste was charmed with Poirot's interest, and was quite inclined to be garrulous.

"That is a splendid specimen there," said Poirot, pointing. "Might I perhaps have a cutting of it?"

"But certainly, monsieur." The old fellow stepped into the bed, and carefully took a slip from the plant Poirot had admired.

Poirot was profuse in his thanks, and Auguste departed to his barrow.

"You see?" said Poirot with a smile, as he bent over the bed to examine the indentation of the gardener's hobnailed boot. "It is quite simple."

"I did not realize—"

"That the foot would be inside the boot? You do not use your excellent mental capacities sufficiently. Well, what of the footmark?"

I examined the bed carefully.

"All the footmarks in the bed were made by the same boot," I said at length after a careful study.

"You think so? *Eh bien*! I agree with you," said Poirot.

He seemed quite uninterested, and as though he were thinking of something else.

"At any rate," I remarked, "you will have one bee less in your bonnet now."

"*Mon Dieu*! But what an idiom! What does it mean?"

"What I meant was that now you will give up your interest in these footmarks."

But to my surprise Poirot shook his head.

"No, no, *mon ami*. At last I am on the right track. I am still in the dark, but, as I hinted just now to Monsieur Bex, these footmarks are the most important and interesting things in the case! That poor Giraud—I should not be surprised if he took no notice of them whatever."

At that moment the front door opened, and M. Hautet and the commissary came down the steps.

"Ah, Monsieur Poirot, we were coming to look for you," said the magistrate. "It is getting late, but I wish to pay a visit to Madame Daubreuil. Without doubt she will be very much upset by Monsieur Renauld's death, and we may be fortunate enough to get a clue from her. The secret that he did not confide to his wife, it is possible that he may have told it to the woman whose love held him enslaved. We know where our Samsons are weak, don't we?"

We said no more, but fell into line. Poirot walked with the examining magistrate, and the commissary and I followed a few paces behind.

"There is no doubt that Françoise's story is substantially correct," he remarked to me in a confidential tone. "I have been telephoning headquarters. It seems that three times in the last six weeks—that is to say since the arrival of Monsieur Renauld at Merlinville—Madame

Daubreuil has paid a large sum in notes into her banking account. Altogether the sum totals two hundred thousand francs!"

"Dear me," I said, considering, "that must be something like four thousand pounds!"

"Precisely. Yes, there can be no doubt that he was absolutely infatuated. But it remains to be seen whether he confided his secret to her. The examining magistrate is hopeful, but I hardly share his views."

During this conversation we were walking down the lane towards the fork in the road where our car had halted earlier in the afternoon, and in another moment I realized that the Villa Marguerite, the home of the mysterious Madame Daubreuil, was the small house from which the beautiful girl had emerged.

"She has lived here for many years," said the commissary nodding his head towards the house. "Very quietly, very unobtrusively. She seems to have no friends or relations other than the acquaintances she has made in Merlinville. She never refers to the past, nor to her husband. One does not even know if he is alive or dead. There is a mystery about her, you comprehend."

I nodded, my interest growing.

"And—the daughter?" I ventured.

"A truly beautiful young girl—modest, devout, all that she should be. One pities her, for, though she may know nothing of the past, a man who wants to ask her hand in marriage must necessarily inform himself, and then—" The commissary shrugged his shoulders cynically.

"But it would not be her fault!" I cried, with rising indignation.

"No. But what will you? A man is particular about his wife's antecedents."

I was prevented from further argument by our arrival at the door. M. Hautet rang the bell. A few minutes elapsed, and then we heard a footfall within, and the door was opened. On the threshold stood my young goddess of that afternoon. When she saw us, the colour left her cheeks, leaving her deathly white, and her eyes widened with apprehension. There was no doubt about it, she was afraid!

"Mademoiselle Daubreuil," said M. Hautet, sweeping off his hat, "we regret infinitely to disturb you, but the exigencies of the Law, you comprehend? My compliments to madame your mother, and will she have the goodness to grant me a few moments' interview?"

For a moment the girl stood motionless. Her left hand was pressed to her side, as though to still the sudden unconquerable agitation of her heart. But she mastered herself, and said in a low voice:

"I will go and see. Please come inside."

She entered a room on the left of the hall, and we heard the low murmur of her voice. And then another voice, much the same in timbre, but with a slightly harder inflection behind its mellow roundness, said:

"But certainly. Ask them to enter."

In another minute we were face to face with the mysterious Madame Daubreuil.

She was not nearly so tall as her daughter, and the rounded curves of her figure had all the grace of full maturity. Her hair, again unlike her daughter's, was dark, and parted in the middle in the Madonna style. Her eyes, half hidden by the drooping lids, were blue. Though very well-preserved, she was certainly no longer young, but her charm was of the quality which is independent of age.

"You wished to see me, monsieur?" she asked.

"Yes, madame." M. Hautet cleared his throat. "I am investigating the death of Monsieur Renauld. You have heard of it, no doubt?"

She bowed her head without speaking. Her expression did not change.

"We came to ask you whether you can—er—throw any light upon the circumstances surrounding it?"

"I?" The surprise of her tone was excellent.

"Yes, madame. We have reason to believe that you were in the habit of visiting the dead man at his villa in the evenings. Is that so?"

The colour rose in the lady's pale cheeks, but she replied quietly:

"I deny your right to ask me such a question!"

"Madame, we are investigating a murder."

"Well, what of it? I had nothing to do with the murder."

"Madame, we do not say that for a moment. But you knew the dead man well. Did he ever confide in you as to any danger that threatened him?"

"Never."

"Did he ever mention his life in Santiago, and any enemies he may have made there?"

"No."

"Then you can give us no help at all?"

"I fear not. I really do not see why you should come to me. Cannot his wife tell you what you want to know?" Her voice held a slender inflection of irony.

"Mrs. Renauld has told us all she can."

"Ah!" said Madame Daubreuil. "I wonder—"

"You wonder what, madame?"

"Nothing."

The examining magistrate looked at her. He was aware that he was fighting a duel, and that he had no mean antagonist.

"You persist in your statement that Monsieur Renauld confided nothing to you?"

"Why should you think it likely that he should confide in me?"

"Because, madame," said M. Hautet, with calculated brutality, "a man tells to his mistress what he does not always tell to his wife."

"Ah!" She sprang forward. Her eyes flashed

fire. "Monsieur, you insult me! And before my daughter! I can tell you nothing. Have the goodness to leave my house!"

The honours undoubtedly rested with the lady. We left the Villa Marguerite like a shamefaced pack of schoolboys. The magistrate muttered angry ejaculations to himself. Poirot seemed lost in thought. Suddenly he came out of his reverie with a start, and inquired of M. Hautet if there was a good hotel near at hand.

"There is a small place, the Hôtel des Bains, on this side of the town. A few hundred yards down the road. It will be handy for your investigations. We shall see you in the morning, then, I presume?"

"Yes, I thank you, Monsieur Hautet."

With mutual civilities we parted company, Poirot and I going towards Merlinville, and the others returning to the Villa Geneviève.

"The French police system is very marvellous," said Poirot, looking after them. "The information they possess about everyone's life, down to the most commonplace detail, is extraordinary. Though he has only been here a little over six weeks, they are perfectly well acquainted with Monsieur Renauld's tastes and pursuits, and at a moment's notice they can produce information as to Madame Daubreuil's banking account, and the sums that have lately been paid in! Undoubtedly the dossier is a great institution. But what is that?" He turned sharply.

A figure was running hatless down the road after us. It was Marthe Daubreuil.

"I beg your pardon," she cried breathlessly, as she reached us. "I—I should not do this, I know. You must not tell my mother. But is it true, what the people say, that Monsieur Renauld called in a detective before he died, and—and that you are he?"

"Yes, mademoiselle," said Poirot gently. "It is quite true. But how did you learn it?"

"Françoise told our Amélie," explained Marthe with a blush.

Poirot made a grimace.

"The secrecy, it is impossible in an affair of this kind! Not that it matters. Well, mademoiselle, what is it you want to know?"

The girl hesitated. She seemed longing, yet fearing, to speak. At last, almost in a whisper, she asked:

"Is—anyone suspected?"

Poirot eyed her keenly.

Then he replied evasively:

"Suspicion is in the air at present, mademoiselle."

"Yes, I know—but—anyone in particular?"

"Why do you want to know?"

The girl seemed frightened by the question. All at once Poirot's words about her earlier in the day occurred to me. The "girl with the anxious eyes."

"Monsieur Renauld was always very kind to

me," she replied at last. "It is natural that I should be interested."

"I see," said Poirot. "Well, mademoiselle, suspicion at present is hovering round two persons."

"Two?"

I could have sworn there was a note of surprise and relief in her voice.

"Their names are unknown, but they are presumed to be Chileans from Santiago. And now, mademoiselle, you see what comes of being young and beautiful! I have betrayed professional secrets for you!"

The girl laughed merrily, and then, rather shyly, she thanked him."

"I must run back now. *Maman* will miss me."

And she turned and ran back up the road, looking like a modern Atalanta. I stared after her.

"*Mon ami*," said Poirot, in his gentle ironical voice, "is it that we are to remain planted here all night—just because you have seen a beautiful young woman, and your head is in a whirl."

I laughed and apologized.

"But she *is* beautiful, Poirot. Anyone might be excused for being bowled over by her."

But to my surprise Poirot shook his head very earnestly.

"Ah, *mon ami*, do not set your heart on Marthe Daubreuil. She is not for you, that one! Take it from Papa Poirot!"

"Why," I cried, "the commissary assured me that she was as good as she is beautiful! A perfect angel!"

"Some of the greatest criminals I have known had the faces of angels," remarked Poirot cheerfully. "A malformation of the grey cells may coincide quite easily with the face of a Madonna."

"Poirot," I cried, horrified, "you cannot mean that you suspect an innocent child like this!"

"Ta-ta-ta! Do not excite yourself! I have not said that I suspected her. But you must admit that her anxiety to know about the case is somewhat unusual."

"For once I see farther than you do," I said. "Her anxiety is not for herself—but for her mother."

"My friend," said Poirot, "as usual, you see nothing at all. Madame Daubreuil is very well able to look after herself without her daughter worrying about her. I admit I was teasing you just now, but all the same I repeat what I said before. Do not set your heart on that girl. She is not for you! I, Hercule Poirot, know it. *Sacré*! if only I could remember where I had seen that face?"

"What face?" I asked, surprised. "The daughter's?"

"No. The mother's."

Noting my surprise, he nodded emphatically.

"But yes—it is as I tell you. It was a long time

ago, when I was still with the police in Belgium. I have never actually seen the woman before, but I have seen her picture—and in connexion with some case. I rather fancy—"

"Yes?"

"I may be mistaken, but I rather fancy that it was a murder case!"

Eight

AN UNEXPECTED MEETING

We were up at the villa betimes next morning. The man on guard at the gate did not bar our way this time. Instead, he respectfully saluted us, and we passed on to the house. The maid Léonie was just coming down the stairs, and seemed not averse to the prospect of a little conversation.

Poirot inquired after the health of Mrs. Renauld.

Léonie shook her head.

"She is terribly upset, the poor lady! She will eat nothing—but nothing! And she is as pale as a ghost. It is heartrending to see her. Ah, it is not I who would grieve like that for a man who had deceived me with another woman!"

Poirot nodded sympathetically.

"What you say is very just, but what will you? The heart of a woman who loves will forgive many blows. Still undoubtedly there must have been many scenes of recrimination between them in the last few months?"

Again Léonie shook her head.

"Never, monsieur. Never have I heard madame utter a word of protest—of reproach, even! She had the temper and disposition of an angel—quite different to monsieur."

"Monsieur Renauld had not the temper of an angel?"

"Far from it. When he enraged himself, the whole house knew of it. The day that he quarrelled with Monsieur Jack—*ma foi*! they might have been heard in the marketplace, they shouted so loud!"

"Indeed," said Poirot. "And when did this quarrel take place?"

"Oh, it was just before Monsieur Jack went to Paris. Almost he missed his train. He came out of the library, and caught up his bag which he had left in the hall. The automobile, it was being repaired, and he had to run for the station. I was dusting the *salon*, and I saw him pass, and his face was white—white—with two burning spots of red. Ah, but he was angry!"

Léonie was enjoying her narrative thoroughly.

"And the dispute, what was it about?"

"Ah, that I do not know," confessed Léonie. "It is true that they shouted, but their voices were so loud and high, and they spoke so fast, that only one well acquainted with English could have comprehended. But monsieur, he was like a thundercloud all day! Impossible to please him!"

The sound of a door shutting upstairs cut short Léonie's loquacity.

"And Françoise who awaits me!" she exclaimed, awakening to a tardy remembrance of her duties. "That old one, she always scolds."

"One moment, mademoiselle. The examining magistrate, where is he?"

"They have gone out to look at the automobile in the garage. Monsieur the commissary had some idea that it might have been used on the night of the murder."

"*Quelle idée*," murmured Poirot, as the girl disappeared.

"You will go out and join them?"

"No, I shall await their return in the *salon*. It is cool there on this hot morning."

This placid way of taking things did not quite commend itself to me.

"If you don't mind—" I said, and hesitated.

"Not in the least. You wish to investigate on your own account, eh?"

"Well, I'd rather like to have a look at Giraud, if he's anywhere about, and see what he's up to."

"The human foxhound," murmured Poirot, as he leaned back in a comfortable chair, and closed his eyes. "By all means, my friend. Au revoir."

I strolled out of the front door. It was certainly hot. I turned up the path we had taken the day before. I had a mind to study the scene of the crime myself. I did not go directly to the spot, however, but turned aside into the bushes, so as to come out on the links some hundred yards or so farther to the right. The shrubbery here was much denser, and I had quite a struggle to force my way through. When I emerged at last on the course, it was quite unexpectedly and with such vigour that I cannoned heavily into a young lady who had been standing with her back to the plantation.

She not unnaturally gave a suppressed shriek, but I, too, uttered an exclamation of surprise. For it was my friend of the train, Cinderella!

The surprise was mutual.

"You!" we both exclaimed simultaneously.

The young lady recovered herself first.

"My only aunt!" she exclaimed. "What are you doing here?"

"For the matter of that, what are you?" I retorted.

"When last I saw you, the day before yesterday, you were trotting home to England like a good little boy."

"When last I saw *you*," I said, "you were trotting home with your sister, like a good little girl. By the way, how is your sister?"

A flash of white teeth rewarded me.

"How kind of you to ask! My sister is well, I thank you."

"She is here with you?"

"She remained in town," said the minx with dignity.

"I don't believe you've got a sister," I laughed. "If you have, her name is Harris!"

"Do you remember mine?" she asked with a smile.

"Cinderella. But you're going to tell me the real one now aren't you?"

She shook her head with a wicked look.

"Not even why you're here?"

"Oh, *that!* I suppose you've heard of members of my profession 'resting.'"

"At expensive French watering places?"

"Dirt cheap if you know where to go."

I eyed her keenly.

"Still, you'd no intention of coming here when I met you two days ago?"

"We all have our disappointments," said Miss Cinderella sententiously. "There now, I've told you quite as much as is good for you. Little boys should not be inquisitive. You've not yet told me what *you're* doing here?"

"You remember my telling you that my great friend was a detective?"

"Yes?"

"And perhaps you've heard about this crime—at the Villa Geneviève—?"

She stared at me. Her breast heaved, and her eyes grew wide and round.

"You don't mean—that you're in on *that?*"

I nodded. There was no doubt that I had scored heavily. Her emotion, as she regarded me, was only too evident. For some few seconds she remained silent, staring at me. Then she nodded her head emphatically.

"Well, if that doesn't beat the band! Tote me round. I want to see all the horrors."

"What do you mean?"

"What I say. Bless the boy, didn't I tell you I doted on crimes? I've been nosing round for hours. It's a real piece of luck happening on you this way. Come on, show me all the sights."

"But look here—wait a minute—I can't. Nobody's allowed in. They're awfully strict."

"Aren't you and your friends the big bugs?"

I was loath to relinquish my position of importance.

"Why are you so keen?" I asked weakly. "And what is it you want to see?"

"Oh, everything! The place where it happened, and the weapon, and the body, and any fingerprints or interesting things like that. I've never had a chance before of being right in on a murder like this. It'll last me all my life."

I turned away, sickened. What were women coming to nowadays? The girl's ghoulish excitement nauseated me.

"Come off your high horse," said the lady suddenly. "And don't give yourself airs. When you got called to this job, did you put your nose in the air and say it was a nasty business, and you wouldn't be mixed-up in it?"

"No, but—"

"If you'd been here on a holiday, wouldn't you be nosing round just the same as I am? Of course you would."

"I'm a man. You're a woman."

"Your idea of a woman is someone who gets on a chair and shrieks if she sees a mouse. That's all prehistoric. But you *will* show me round, won't you? You see, it might make a big difference to me."

"In what way?"

"They're keeping all the reporters out. I might make a big scoop with one of the papers. You don't know how much they pay for a bit of inside stuff."

I hesitated. She slipped a small soft hand into mine.

"*Please*—there's a dear."

I capitulated. Secretly, I knew that I should rather enjoy the part of showman.

We repaired first to the spot where the body had been discovered. A man was on guard there, who saluted respectfully, knowing me by sight, and raised no questions as to my companion. Presumably he regarded her as vouched for by me. I explained to Cinderella just how the discovery had been made, and she listened attentively, sometimes putting an intelligent question. Then we turned our steps in the direction of the villa. I proceeded rather cautiously, for, truth to tell, I was not at all anxious to meet anyone. I took the girl through the shrubbery round to the back of the house where the small shed was. I recollected that yesterday evening, after relocking the door, M. Bex had left the key with the *sergent de ville*, Marchaud, "In case Monsieur Giraud should require it while we are upstairs." I thought it quite likely that the Sûreté detective, after using it, had returned it to Marchaud again. Leaving the girl out of sight in the shrubbery, I entered the house. Marchaud was on duty outside the door of the *salon*. From within came the murmur of voices.

"Monsieur desires Monsieur Hautet? He is within. He is again interrogating Françoise."

"No," I said hastily, "I don't want him. But I should very much like the key of the shed outside if it is not against regulations."

"But certainly, monsieur." He produced it. "Here it is. Monsieur Hautet gave orders that all facilities were to be placed at your disposal. You will return it to me when you have finished out there, that is all."

"Of course."

I felt a thrill of satisfaction as I realized that in Marchaud's eyes, at least, I ranked equally in importance with Poirot. The girl was waiting for me. She gave an exclamation of delight as she saw the key in my hand.

"You've got it then?"

"Of course," I said coolly. "All the same, you know, what I'm doing is highly irregular."

"You've been a perfect duck, and I shan't forget it. Come along. They can't see us from the house, can they?"

"Wait a minute." I arrested her eager advance. "I won't stop you if you really wish to go in. But do you? You've seen the grave, and the grounds, and you've heard all the details of the affair. Isn't that enough for you? This is going to be gruesome, you know, and—unpleasant."

She looked at me for a moment with an expression that I could not quite fathom. Then she laughed.

"Me for the horrors," she said. "Come along."

In silence we arrived at the door of the shed. I opened it and we passed in. I walked over to the body, and gently pulled down the sheet as Bex had done the preceding afternoon. A little gasping sound escaped from the girl's lips, and I turned and looked at her. There was horror on her face now, and those debonair high spirits of hers were quenched utterly. She had not chosen to listen to my advice, and she was punished now for her disregard of it. I felt singularly merciless towards her. She should go through with it now. I turned the corpse over gently.

"You see," I said. "He was stabbed in the back."
Her voice was almost soundless.

"With what?"

I nodded towards the glass jar.

"That dagger."

Suddenly the girl reeled, and then sank down in a heap. I sprang to her assistance.

"You are faint. Come out of here. It has been too much for you."

"Water," she murmured. "Quick. Water."

I left her, and rushed into the house. Fortunately none of the servants were about, and I was able to secure a glass of water unobserved and add a few drops of brandy from a pocket flask. In a few minutes I was back again. The girl was lying as I had left her, but a few sips of the brandy and water revived her in a marvellous manner.

"Take me out of here—oh, quickly, quickly!" she cried, shuddering.

Supporting her with my arm, I led her out into the air, and she pulled the door to behind her. Then she drew a deep breath.

"That's better. Oh, it was horrible! Why did you ever let me go in?"

I felt this to be so feminine that I could not forbear a smile. Secretly, I was not dissatisfied with her collapse. It proved that she was not quite so callous as I had thought her. After all she was little more than a child, and her curiosity had probably been of the unthinking order.

"I did my best to stop you, you know," I said gently.

"I suppose you did. Well, good-bye."

"Look here, you can't start off like that—all alone. You're not fit for it. I insist on accompanying you back to Merlinville."

"Nonsense. I'm quite all right now."

"Supposing you felt faint again? No, I shall come with you."

But this she combated with a good deal of energy. In the end, however, I prevailed so far as to be allowed to accompany her to the outskirts of the town. We retraced our steps over our former route, passing the grave again, and making a detour on to the road. Where the first straggling line of shops began, she stopped and held out her hand.

"Good-bye, and thank you ever so much for coming with me."

"Are you sure you're all right now?"

"Quite, thanks. I hope you don't get into any trouble over showing me things."

I disclaimed the idea lightly.

"Well, good-bye."

"Au revoir," I corrected. "If you're staying here, we shall meet again."

She flashed a smile at me.

"That's so. Au revoir, then."

"Wait a second, you haven't told me your address."

"Oh, I'm staying at the Hôtel du Phare. It's a little place, but quite good. Come and look me up tomorrow."

"I will," I said, with perhaps rather unnecessary *empressement*.

I watched her out of sight, then turned and retraced my steps to the villa. I remembered that I had not relocked the door of the shed. Fortunately no one had noticed the oversight, and turning the key I removed it and returned it to the *sergent de ville*. And, as I did so, it came upon me suddenly that though Cinderella had given me her address I still did not know her name.

Nine

M. Giraud Finds Some Clues

In the *salon* I found the examining magistrate busily interrogating the old gardener, Auguste. Poirot and the commissary, who were both present, greeted me respectively with a smile and a polite bow. I slipped quietly into a seat. M. Hautet was painstaking and meticulous in the extreme, but did not succeed in eliciting anything of importance.

The gardening gloves Auguste admitted to be his. He wore them when handling a certain species of primula plant which was poisonous to some people. He could not say when he had worn them last. Certainly he had not missed them. Where were they kept? Sometimes in one place, sometimes in another. The spade was usually to be found in the small toolshed. Was it locked? Of course it was locked. Where was the key kept? *Parbleu*, it was in the door of course. There was nothing of value to steal. Who would have expected a party of bandits, or assassins? Such things did not happen in Madame la Vicomtesse's time.

M. Hautet signifying that he had finished with him, the old man withdrew, grumbling to the last. Remembering Poirot's unaccountable insistence on the footprints in the flower-beds, I scrutinized him narrowly as he gave his evidence. Either he had nothing to do with the crime or he was a consummate actor. Suddenly, just as he was going out of the door, an idea struck me.

"*Pardon*, Monsieur Hautet," I cried, "but will you permit me to ask him one question?"

"But certainly, monsieur."

Thus encouraged, I turned to Auguste.

"Where do you keep your boots?"

"On my feet," growled the old man. "Where else?"

"But when you go to bed at night?"

"Under my bed."

"But who cleans them?"

"Nobody. Why should they be cleaned? Is it that I promenade myself on the front like a young man? On Sunday I wear the Sunday boots, but otherwise—" He shrugged his shoulders.

I shook my head, discouraged.

"Well, well," said the magistrate, "we do not advance very much. Undoubtedly we are held up until we get the return cable from Santiago. Has anyone seen Giraud? In verity that one lacks politeness! I have a very good mind to send for him and—"

"You will not have to send far."

The quiet voice startled us. Giraud was standing outside looking in through the open window.

He leapt lightly into the room and advanced to the table.

"Here I am, at your service. Accept my excuses for not presenting myself sooner."

"Not at all—not at all!" said the magistrate, rather confused.

"Of course I am only a detective," continued the other. "I know nothing of interrogatories. Were I conducting one, I should be inclined to do so without an open window. Anyone standing outside can so easily hear all that passes. But no matter."

M. Hautet flushed angrily. There was evidently going to be no love lost between the examining magistrate and the detective in charge of the case. They had fallen foul of each other at the start. Perhaps in any event it would have been much the same. To Giraud, all examining magistrates were fools, and to M. Hautet, who took himself seriously, the casual manner of the Paris detective could not fail to give offence.

"*Eh bien*, Monsieur Giraud," said the magistrate rather sharply. "Without doubt you have been employing your time to a marvel! You have the names of the assassins for us, have you not? And also the precise spot where they find themselves now?"

Unmoved by this irony, M. Giraud replied:

"I know at least where they have come from."

Giraud took two small objects from his pocket and laid them down on the table. We crowded round. The objects were very simple ones: the stub of a cigarette and an unlighted match. The detective wheeled round on Poirot.

"What do you see there?" he asked.

There was something almost brutal in his tone. It made my cheeks flush. But Poirot remained unmoved. He shrugged his shoulders.

"A cigarette end and a match."

"And what does that tell you?"

Poirot spread out his hands.

"It tells me—nothing."

"Ah!" said Giraud, in a satisfied voice. "You haven't made a study of these things. That's not an ordinary match—not in this country at least. It's common enough in South America. Luckily it's unlighted. I mightn't have recognized it otherwise. Evidently one of the men threw away

100

his cigarette and lit another, spilling one match out of the box as he did so."

"And the other match?" asked Poirot.

"Which match?"

"The one he *did* light his cigarette with. You have found that also?"

"No."

"Perhaps you didn't search very thoroughly."

"Not search thoroughly—" For a moment it seemed as though the detective was going to break out angrily, but with an effort he controlled himself. "I see you love a joke, Monsieur Poirot. But in any case, match or no match, the cigarette end would be sufficient. It is a South American cigarette with liquorice pectoral paper."

Poirot bowed. The commissary spoke:

"The cigarette end and match might have belonged to Monsieur Renauld. Remember, it is only two years since he returned from South America."

"No," replied the other confidently. "I have already searched among the effects of Monsieur Renauld. The cigarettes he smoked and the matches he used are quite different."

"You do not think it odd," asked Poirot, "that these strangers should come unprovided with a weapon, with gloves, with a spade, and that they should so conveniently find all these things?"

Giraud smiled in a rather superior manner.

"Undoubtedly it is strange. Indeed, without the

theory that I hold, it would be inexplicable."

"Aha!" said M. Hautet. "An accomplice within the house!"

"Or outside it," said Giraud, with a peculiar smile.

"But someone must have admitted them. We cannot allow that, by an unparalleled piece of good fortune, they found the door ajar for them to walk in?"

"The door was opened for them; but it could just as easily be opened from outside—by someone who possessed a key."

"But who *did* possess a key?"

Giraud shrugged his shoulders.

"As for that, no one who possesses one is going to admit the fact if he can help it. But several people *might* have had one. Monsieur Jack Renauld, the son, for instance. It is true that he is on his way to South America, but he might have lost the key or had it stolen from him. Then there is the gardener—he has been here many years. One of the younger servants may have a lover. It is easy to take an impression of a key and have one cut. There are many possibilities. Then there is another person who, I should judge, is exceedingly likely to have such a thing."

"Who is that?"

"Madame Daubreuil," said the detective.

"Eh, eh!" said the magistrate. "So you have heard about that, have you?"

"I hear everything," said Giraud imperturbably.

"There is one thing I could swear you have not heard," said M. Hautet, delighted to be able to show superior knowledge, and without more ado he retailed the story of the mysterious visitor the night before. He also touched on the cheque made out to "Duveen," and finally handed Giraud the letter signed "Bella."

"All very interesting. But my theory remains unaffected."

"And your theory is?"

"For the moment I prefer not to say. Remember, I am only just beginning my investigations."

"Tell me one thing, Monsieur Giraud," said Poirot suddenly. "Your theory allows for the door being opened. It does not explain why it was *left* open. When they departed, would it not have been natural for them to close it behind them? If a *sergent de ville* had chanced to come up to the house, as is sometimes done to see that all is well, they might have been discovered and overtaken almost at once."

"Bah! They forgot it. A mistake, I grant you."

Then, to my surprise, Poirot uttered almost the same words as he had uttered to Bex the previous evening:

"*I do not agree with you.* The door being left open was the result of either design or necessity, and any theory that does not admit that fact is bound to prove vain."

We all regarded the little man with a good deal of astonishment. The confession of ignorance drawn from him over the match end had, I thought, been bound to humiliate him, but here he was self-satisfied as ever, laying down the law to Giraud without a tremor.

The detective twisted his moustache, eyeing my friend in a somewhat bantering fashion.

"You don't agree with me, eh? Well, what strikes you particularly about the case? Let's hear your views."

"One thing presents itself to me as being significant. Tell me, Monsieur Giraud, does nothing strike you as familiar about this case? Is there nothing it reminds you of?"

"Familiar? Reminds me of? I can't say offhand. I don't think so, though."

"You are wrong," said Poirot quietly. "A crime almost precisely similar has been committed before."

"When? And where?"

"Ah, that, unfortunately, I cannot for the moment remember, but I shall do so. I had hoped *you* might be able to assist me."

Giraud snorted incredulously.

"There have been many affairs of masked men. I cannot remember the details of them all. The crimes all resemble each other more or less."

"There is such a thing as the individual touch." Poirot suddenly assumed his lecturing manner, and addressed us collectively. "I am speaking to you now of the psychology of crime. Monsieur Giraud knows quite well that each criminal has his particular method, and that the police, when called in to investigate, say, a case of burglary, can often make a shrewd guess at the offender, simply by the peculiar methods he has employed. (Japp would tell you the same, Hastings.) Man is an unoriginal animal. Unoriginal within the law in his daily respectable life, equally unoriginal outside the law. If a man commits a crime, any other crime he commits will resemble it closely. The English murderer who disposed of his wives in succession by drowning them in their baths was a case in point. Had he varied his methods, he might have escaped detection to this day. But he obeyed the common dictates of human nature, arguing that what had once succeeded would succeed again, and he paid the penalty of his lack of originality."

"And the point of all this?" sneered Giraud.

"That, when you have two crimes precisely similar in design and execution, you find the same brain behind them both. I am looking for that brain, Monsieur Giraud, and I shall find it. Here we have a true clue—a psychological clue. You may know all about cigarettes and match ends, Monsieur Giraud, but I, Hercule Poirot, know the mind of man."

Giraud remained singularly unimpressed.

"For your guidance," continued Poirot, "I will also advise you of one fact which might fail to be brought to your notice. The wristwatch of Madame Renauld, on the day following the tragedy, had gained two hours."

Giraud stared.

"Perhaps it was in the habit of gaining?"

"As a matter of fact, I am told it did."

"Very well, then."

"All the same, two hours is a good deal," said Poirot softly. "Then there is the matter of the footprints in the flower bed."

He nodded his head towards the open window. Giraud took two eager strides, and looked out.

"But I see no footprints?"

"No," said Poirot, straightening a little pile of books on a table. "There are none."

For a moment an almost murderous rage obscured Giraud's face. He took two strides towards his tormentor, but at that moment the salon door was opened, and Marchaud announced:

"Monsieur Stonor, the secretary, has just arrived from England. May he enter?"

Ten

GABRIEL STONOR

The man who now entered the room was a striking figure. Very tall, with a well-knit, athletic frame, and a deeply bronzed face and neck, he dominated the assembly. Even Giraud seemed anaemic beside him. When I knew him better I realized that Gabriel Stonor was quite an unusual personality. English by birth, he had knocked about all over the world. He had shot big game in Africa, travelled in Korea, ranched in California, and traded in the South Sea islands.

His unerring eye picked out M. Hautet.

"The examining magistrate in charge of the case? Pleased to meet you, sir. This is a terrible business. How's Mrs. Renauld? Is she bearing up fairly well? It must have been an awful shock to her."

"Terrible, terrible," said M. Hautet. "Permit me to introduce Monsieur Bex, our commissary of police, Monsieur Giraud of the Sûreté. This gentleman is Monsieur Hercule Poirot. Mr. Renauld sent for him, but he arrived too late to do anything to avert the tragedy. A friend of Monsieur Poirot's, Captain Hastings."

Stonor looked at Poirot with some interest.

"Sent for you, did he?"

"You did not know, then, that Monsieur Renauld contemplated calling a detective?" interposed M. Bex.

"No, I didn't. But it doesn't surprise me a bit."

"Why?"

"Because the old man was rattled. I don't know what it was all about. He didn't confide in me. We weren't on those terms. But rattled he was—and badly."

"H'm!" said M. Hautet. "But you have no notion of the cause?"

"That's what I said, sir."

"You will pardon me, Monsieur Stonor, but we must begin with a few formalities. Your name?"

"Gabriel Stonor."

"How long ago was it that you became secretary to Monsieur Renauld?"

"About two years ago, when he first arrived from South America. I met him through a mutual friend, and he offered me the post. A thundering good boss he was too."

"Did he talk to you much about his life in South America?"

"Yes, a good bit."

"Do you know if he was ever in Santiago?"

"Several times, I believe."

"He never mentioned any special incident that occurred there—anything that might have provoked some vendetta against him?"

"Never."

"Did he speak of any secret that he had acquired while sojourning there?"

"Not that I can remember. But, for all that, there *was* a mystery about him. I've never heard him speak of his boyhood, for instance, or of any incident prior to his arrival in South America. He was a French-Canadian by birth, I believe, but I've never heard him speak of his life in Canada. He could shut up like a clam if he liked."

"So, as far as you know, he had no enemies, and you can give us no clue as to any secret to obtain possession of which he might have been murdered?"

"That's so."

"Monsieur Stonor, have you ever heard the name of Duveen in connexion with Monsieur Renauld?"

"Duveen. Duveen." He tried the name over thoughtfully. "I don't think I have. And yet it seems familiar."

"Do you know a lady, a friend of Monsieur Renauld's, whose Christian name is Bella?"

Again Mr. Stonor shook his head.

"Bella Duveen? Is that the full name? It's curious. I'm sure I know it. But for the moment I can't remember in what connexion."

The magistrate coughed.

"You understand, Monsieur Stonor—the case is like this. *There must be no reservations.* You might, perhaps, through a feeling of consideration for Madame Renauld—for whom, I gather, you have a great esteem and affection—you might—in fact!" said M. Hautet, getting rather tied up in his sentence, "there must absolutely be no reservations."

Stonor stared at him, a dawning light of comprehension in his eyes.

"I don't quite get you," he said gently. "Where does Mrs. Renauld come in? I've an immense respect and affection for that lady; she's a very wonderful and unusual type, but I don't quite see how my reservations, or otherwise, could affect her."

"Not if this Bella Duveen should prove to have been something more than a friend to her husband?"

"Ah!" said Stonor. "I get you now. But I'll bet my bottom dollar that you're wrong. The old man never so much as looked at a petticoat. He just adored his own wife. They were the most devoted couple I know."

M. Hautet shook his head gently.

"Monsieur Stonor, we hold absolute proof—a love letter written by this Bella to Monsieur Renauld, accusing him of having tired of her. Moreover, we have further proof that, at the time of his death, he was carrying on an intrigue with a Frenchwoman, a Madame Daubreuil, who rents the adjoining villa."

The secretary's eyes narrowed.

"Hold on, sir. You're barking up the wrong tree. I knew Paul Renauld. What you've just been saying is plumb impossible. There's some other explanation."

The magistrate shrugged his shoulders.

"What other explanation could there be?"

"What leads you to think it was a love affair?"

"Madame Daubreuil was in the habit of visiting him here in the evenings. Also, since Monsieur Renauld came to the Villa Geneviève, Madame Daubreuil has paid large sums of money into the bank in notes. In all, the amount totals four thousand pounds of your English money."

"I guess that's right," said Stonor quietly. "I transmitted him those sums in notes at his request. But it wasn't an intrigue."

"What else could it be?"

"Blackmail," said Stonor sharply, bringing down his hand with a slam on the table. "That's what it was."

"Ah!" cried the magistrate, shaken in spite of himself.

"Blackmail," repeated Stonor. "The old man was being bled—and at a good rate too. Four thousand in a couple of months. Whew! I told you just now there was a mystery about Renauld. Evidently this Madame Daubreuil knew enough of it to put the screw on."

"It is possible," the commissary cried excitedly. "Decidedly it is possible."

111

"Possible?" roared Stonor. "It's certain. Tell me, have you asked Mrs. Renauld about this love affair stunt of yours?"

"No, monsieur. We did not wish to occasion her any distress if it could reasonably be avoided."

"Distress? Why, she'd laugh in your face. I tell you, she and Renauld were a couple in a hundred."

"Ah, that reminds me of another point," said M. Hautet. "Did Monsieur Renauld take you into his confidence at all as to the dispositions of his will?"

"I know all about it—took it to the lawyers for him after he'd drawn it out. I can give you the name of his solicitors if you want to see it. They've got it there. Quite simple. Half in trust to his wife for her lifetime, the other half to his son. A few legacies. I rather think he left me a thousand."

"When was this will drawn up?"

"Oh, about a year and a half ago."

"Would it surprise you very much, Monsieur Stonor, to hear that Monsieur Renauld had made another will, less than a fortnight ago?"

Stonor was obviously very much surprised.

"I'd no idea of it. What's it like?"

"The whole of his vast fortune is left unreservedly to his wife. There is no mention of his son."

Mr. Stonor gave vent to a prolonged whistle.

"I call that rather rough on the lad. His mother adores him of course, but to the world at large it looks rather like a want of confidence on his father's part. It will be rather galling to his pride. Still, it all goes to prove what I told you, that Renauld and his wife were on first-rate terms."

"Quite so, quite so," said M. Hautet. "It is possible we shall have to revise our ideas on several points. We have, of course, cabled to Santiago, and are expecting a reply from there any minute. In all probability, everything will then be perfectly clear and straightforward. On the other hand, if your suggestion of blackmail is true, Madame Daubreuil ought to be able to give us valuable information."

Poirot interjected a remark:

"Monsieur Stonor, the English chauffeur, Masters, had he been long with Monsieur Renauld?"

"Over a year."

"Have you any idea whether he has ever been in South America?"

"I'm quite sure he hasn't. Before coming to M. Renauld he had been for many years with some people in Gloucestershire whom I know well."

"In fact, you can answer for him as being above suspicion?"

"Absolutely."

Poirot seemed somewhat crestfallen.

Meanwhile the magistrate had summoned Marchaud.

"My compliments to Madame Renauld, and I should be glad to speak to her for a few minutes. Beg her not to disturb herself. I will wait upon her upstairs."

Marchaud saluted and disappeared.

We waited some minutes, and then, to our surprise, the door opened, and Mrs. Renauld, deathly pale in her heavy mourning, entered the room.

M. Hautet brought forward a chair, uttering vigorous protestations, and she thanked him with a smile. Stonor was holding one hand of hers in his with an eloquent sympathy. Words evidently failed him. Mrs. Renauld turned to M. Hautet.

"You wish to ask me something?"

"With your permission, madame. I understand your husband was a French-Canadian by birth. Can you tell me anything of his youth or upbringing?"

She shook her head.

"My husband was always very reticent about himself, monsieur. He came from the North-West, I know, but I fancy that he had an unhappy childhood, for he never cared to speak of that time. Our life was lived entirely in the present and the future."

"Was there any mystery in his past life?"

Mrs. Renauld smiled a little and shook her head.

"Nothing so romantic, I am sure, monsieur."

M. Hautet also smiled.

"True, we must not permit ourselves to get melodramatic. There is one thing more—" He hesitated.

Stonor broke in impetuously:

"They've got an extraordinary idea into their heads, Mrs. Renauld. They actually fancy that Mr. Renauld was carrying on an intrigue with a Madame Daubreuil who, it seems, lives next door."

The scarlet colour flamed into Mrs. Renauld's cheeks. She flung her head up, then bit her lip, her face quivering. Stonor stood looking at her in astonishment, but M. Bex leaned forward and said gently:

"We regret to cause you pain, madame, but have you any reason to believe that Madame Daubreuil was your husband's mistress?"

With a sob of anguish, Mrs. Renauld buried her face in her hands. Her shoulders heaved convulsively. At last she lifted her head and said brokenly:

"She may have been."

Never, in all my life, have I seen anything to equal the blank amazement on Stonor's face. He was thoroughly taken aback.

Eleven

JACK RENAULD

What the next development of the conversation would have been I cannot say, for at that moment the door was thrown open violently and a tall young man strode into the room.

Just for a moment I had the uncanny sensation that the dead man had come to life again. Then I realized that this dark head was untouched with grey, and that, in point of fact, it was a mere boy who now burst in among us with so little ceremony. He went straight to Mrs. Renauld with an impetuosity that took no heed of the presence of others.

"Mother!"

"Jack!" With a cry she folded him in her arms. "My dearest! But what brings you here? You were to sail on the *Anzora* from Cherbourg two days ago?" Then, suddenly recalling to herself the presence of others, she turned with a certain dignity: "My son, messieurs."

"Aha!" said M. Hautet, acknowledging the young man's bow. "So you did not sail on the *Anzora*?"

"No, monsieur. As I was about to explain, the *Anzora* was detained twenty-four hours through engine trouble. I should have sailed last night

116

instead of the night before, but, happening to buy an evening paper, I saw in it an account of the—the awful tragedy that had befallen us—" His voice broke and the tears came into his eyes. "My poor father—my poor, poor father."

Staring at him like one in a dream, Mrs. Renauld repeated:

"So you did not sail?" And then, with a gesture of infinite weariness, she murmured as though to herself: "After all, it does not matter—now."

"Sit down, Monsieur Renauld, I beg of you," said M. Hautet, indicating a chair. "My sympathy for you is profound. It must have been a terrible shock to you to learn the news as you did. However, it is most fortunate that you were prevented from sailing. I am in hopes that you may be able to give us just the information we need to clear up this mystery."

"I am at your disposal, monsieur. Ask me any questions you please."

"To begin with, I understand that this journey was being undertaken at your father's request?"

"Quite so, monsieur. I received a telegram bidding me to proceed without delay to Buenos Aires, and from thence *via* the Andes to Valparaiso, and on to Santiago."

"Ah! And the object of this journey?"

"I have no idea."

"What?"

"No. See, here in the telegram."

The magistrate took it and read it aloud:

" 'Proceed immediately Cherbourg embark *Anzora* sailing tonight Buenos Aires. Ultimate destination Santiago. Further instructions will await you Buenos Aires. Do not fail. Matter is of utmost importance. Renauld.' And there had been no previous correspondence on the matter?"

Jack Renauld shook his head.

"That is the only intimation of any kind. I knew, of course, that my father, having lived so long out there, had necessarily many interests in South America. But he had never mooted any suggestion of sending me out."

"You have, of course, been a good deal in South America, M. Renauld?"

"I was there as a child. But I was educated in England, and spent most of my holidays in that country, so I really know far less of South America than might be supposed. You see, the War broke out when I was seventeen."

"You served in the English Flying Corps, did you not?"

"Yes, monsieur."

M. Hautet nodded his head and proceeded with his inquiries along the, by now, well-known lines. In response, Jack Renauld declared definitely that he knew nothing of any enmity his father might have incurred in the city of Santiago or elsewhere in the South American continent, that he had noticed no change in his father's

118

manner of late, and that he had never heard him refer to a secret. He had regarded the mission to South America as connected with business interests.

As M. Hautet paused for a minute, the quiet voice of Giraud broke in:

"I should like to put a few questions of my own, Monsieur le juge."

"By all means, Monsieur Giraud, if you wish," said the magistrate coldly.

Giraud edged his chair a little nearer to the table.

"Were you on good terms with your father, Monsieur Renauld?"

"Certainly I was," returned the lad haughtily.

"You assert that positively?"

"Yes."

"No little disputes, eh?"

Jack shrugged his shoulders. "Everyone may have a difference of opinion now and then."

"Quite so, quite so. But, if anyone were to assert that you had a violent quarrel with your father on the eve of your departure for Paris, that person, without doubt, would be lying?"

I could not but admire the ingenuity of Giraud. His boast, "I know everything," had been no idle one. Jack Renauld was clearly disconcerted by the question.

"We—we did have an argument," he admitted.

"Ah, an argument! In the course of that

argument, did you use this phrase: 'When you are dead I can do as I please?'"

"I may have done," muttered the other. "I don't know."

"In response to that, did your father say: 'But I am not dead yet!?' To which you responded: 'I wish you were!'"

The boy made no answer. His hands fiddled nervously with the things on the table in front of him.

"I must request an answer, please, Monsieur Renauld," said Giraud sharply.

With an angry exclamation, the boy swept a heavy paper knife to the floor.

"What does it matter? You might as well know. Yes, I did quarrel with my father. I dare say I said all those things—I was so angry I cannot even remember what I said! I was furious—I could almost have killed him at that moment—there, make the most of that!" He leant back in his chair, flushed and defiant.

Giraud smiled, then, moving his chair back a little, said:

"That is all. You would, without doubt, prefer to continue the interrogatory, Monsieur Hautet."

"Ah, yes, exactly," said M. Hautet. "And what was the subject of your quarrel?"

"That I decline to state."

M. Hautet sat up in his chair.

"Monsieur Renauld, it is not permitted to trifle

with the law!" he thundered. "What was the subject of the quarrel?"

Young Renauld remained silent, his boyish face sullen and overcast. But another voice spoke, imperturbable and calm, the voice of Hercule Poirot:

"I will inform you, if you like, monsieur."

"You know?"

"Certainly I know. The subject of the quarrel was Mademoiselle Marthe Daubreuil."

Renauld sprang round, startled. The magistrate leaned forward.

"Is that so, monsieur?"

Jack Renauld bowed his head.

"Yes," he admitted. "I love Mademoiselle Daubreuil, and I wish to marry her. When I informed my father of the fact he flew at once into a violent rage. Naturally, I could not stand hearing the girl I loved insulted, and I, too, lost my temper."

M. Hautet looked across at Mrs. Renauld.

"You were aware of this—attachment, madame?"

"I feared it," she replied simply.

"Mother," cried the boy. "You too! Marthe is as good as she is beautiful. What can you have against her?"

"I have nothing against Mademoiselle Daubreuil in any way. But I should prefer you to marry an Englishwoman, or if a Frenchwoman,

121

not one who has a mother of doubtful antecedents!"

Her rancour against the older woman showed plainly in her voice, and I could well understand that it must have been a bitter blow to her when her only son showed signs of falling in love with the daughter of her rival.

Mrs. Renauld continued, addressing the magistrate:

"I ought, perhaps, to have spoken to my husband on the subject, but I hoped that it was only a boy and girl flirtation which would blow over all the quicker if no notice was taken of it. I blame myself now for my silence, but my husband, as I told you, had seemed so anxious and careworn, different altogether from his normal self, that I was chiefly concerned not to give him any additional worry."

M. Hautet nodded.

"When you informed your father of your intentions towards Mademoiselle Daubreuil," he resumed, "he was surprised?"

"He seemed completely taken aback. Then he ordered me peremptorily to dismiss any such idea from my mind. He would never give his consent to such a marriage. Nettled, I demanded what he had against Mademoiselle Daubreuil. To that he could give no satisfactory reply, but spoke in slighting terms of the mystery surrounding the lives of the mother and daughter. I answered that

I was marrying Marthe and not her antecedents, but he shouted me down with a peremptory refusal to discuss the matter in any way. The whole thing must be given up. The injustice and high-handedness of it all maddened me—especially since he himself always seemed to go out of his way to be attentive to the Daubreuils and was always suggesting that they should be asked to the house. I lost my head, and we quarrelled in earnest. My father reminded me that I was entirely dependent on him, and it must have been in answer to that that I made the remark about doing as I pleased after his death—"

Poirot interrupted with a quick question:

"You were aware, then, of the terms of your father's will?"

"I knew that he had left half his fortune to me, the other half in trust for my mother, to come to me at her death," replied the lad.

"Proceed with your story," said the magistrate.

"After that we shouted at each other in sheer rage, until I suddenly realized that I was in danger of missing my train to Paris. I had to run for the station, still in a white heat of fury. However, once well away, I calmed down. I wrote to Marthe, telling her what had happened, and her reply soothed me still further. She pointed out to me that we had only to be steadfast, and any opposition was bound to give way at last. Our affection for each other must be tried and proved, and when my parents realized that it was no light infatuation on my part they would doubtless relent towards us. Of course, to her, I had not dwelt on my father's principal objection to the match. I soon saw that I should do my cause no good by violence."

"To pass to another matter, are you acquainted with the name of Duveen, Monsieur Renauld?"

"Duveen?" said Jack. "Duveen?" He leant forward and slowly picked up the paper knife he had swept from the table. As he lifted his head his eyes met the watching ones of Giraud. "Duveen? No, I can't say I do."

"Will you read this letter, Monsieur Renauld? And tell me if you have any idea as to who the person was who addressed it to your father."

Jack Renauld took the letter and read it through, the colour mounting in his face as he did so.

"Addressed to my father?" The emotion and indignation in his tones were evident.

"Yes. We found it in the pocket of his coat."

"Does—" He hesitated, throwing the merest fraction of a glance towards his mother.

The magistrate understood.

"As yet—no. Can you give us any clue as to the writer?"

"I have no idea whatsoever."

M. Hautet sighed.

"A most mysterious case. Ah, well, I suppose we can now rule out the letter altogether. Let me see, where were we? Oh, the weapon. I fear this may give you pain, Monsieur Renauld. I understand it was a present from you to your mother. Very sad—very distressing—"

Jack Renauld leaned forward. His face, which had flushed during the perusal of the letter, was now deadly white.

"Do you mean—that it was with an aeroplane wire paper-cutter that my father was—was killed? But it's impossible! A little thing like that!"

"Alas, Monsieur Renauld, it is only too true! An ideal little tool, I fear. Sharp and easy to handle."

"Where is it? Can I see it? Is it still in the—the body?"

"Oh no, it has been removed. You would like to see it? To make sure? It would be as well, perhaps, though madame has already identified it. Still—Monsieur Bex, might I trouble you?"

"Certainly. I will fetch it immediately."

"Would it not be better to take Monsieur Renauld to the shed?" suggested Giraud smoothly. "Without doubt he would wish to see his father's body."

The boy made a shivering gesture of negation, and the magistrate, always disposed to cross Giraud whenever possible, replied:

"But no—not at present. Monsieur Bex will be so kind as to bring it to us here."

The commissary left the room. Stonor crossed to Jack and wrung him by the hand. Poirot had risen, and was adjusting a pair of candlesticks that struck his trained eye as being a shade askew. The magistrate was reading the mysterious love letter through a last time, clinging desperately to his first theory of jealousy and a stab in the back.

Suddenly the door burst open and the commissary rushed in.

"Monsieur le juge! Monsieur le juge!"

"But yes. What is it?"

"The dagger! It is gone!"

"What—gone?"

"Vanished. Disappeared. The glass jar that contained it is empty!"

"What?" I cried. "Impossible. Why, only this morning I saw—" The words died on my tongue.

But the attention of the entire room was diverted to me.

"What is that you say?" cried the commissary. "This morning?"

"I saw it there this morning," I said slowly. "About an hour and a half ago, to be accurate."

"You went to the shed, then? How did you get the key?"

"I asked the *sergent de ville* for it."

"And you went there? Why?"

I hesitated, but in the end I decided that the only thing to do was to make a clean breast of it.

"Monsieur Hautet," I said, "I have committed a grave fault, for which I must crave your indulgence."

"Proceed, monsieur."

"The fact of the matter is," I said, wishing myself anywhere else but where I was, "that I met a young lady, an acquaintance of mine. She displayed a great desire to see everything that was to be seen, and I—well, in short, I took the key to show her the body."

"Ah!" cried the magistrate indignantly. "But it is a grave fault you have committed there, Captain Hastings. It is altogether most irregular. You should not have permitted yourself this folly."

"I know," I said meekly. "Nothing that you can say could be too severe, monsieur."

"You did not invite this lady to come here?"

"Certainly not. I met her quite by accident. She is an English lady who happens to be staying in Merlinville, though I was not aware of that until my unexpected meeting with her."

"Well, well," said the magistrate, softening. "It was most irregular, but the lady is without doubt young and beautiful. What it is to be young!" And he sighed sentimentally.

But the commissary, less romantic and more practical, took up the tale:

"But did you not reclose and lock the door when you departed?"

"That's just it," I said slowly. "That's what I blame myself for so terribly. My friend was upset at the sight. She nearly fainted. I got her some brandy and water, and afterwards insisted on accompanying her back to the town. In the excitement I forgot to relock the door. I only did so when I got back to the villa."

"Then for twenty minutes at least—" said the commissary slowly. He stopped.

"Exactly," I said.

"Twenty minutes," mused the commissary.

"It is deplorable," said M. Hautet, his sternness of manner returning. "Without precedent."

Suddenly another voice spoke.

"You find it deplorable?" asked Giraud.

"Certainly I do."

"I find it admirable!" said the other imperturbably.

This unexpected ally quite bewildered me.

"Admirable, Monsieur Giraud?" asked the magistrate, studying him cautiously out of the corner of his eye.

"Precisely."

"And why?"

"Because we know now that the assassin, or an accomplice of the assassin, has been near the villa only an hour ago. It will be strange if, with that knowledge, we do not shortly lay hands upon him." There was a note of menace in his voice. He continued: "He risked a good deal to gain possession of that dagger. Perhaps he feared that fingerprints might be discovered on it."

Poirot turned to Bex.

"You said there were none?"

Giraud shrugged his shoulders.

"Perhaps he could not be sure."

Poirot looked at him.

"You are wrong, Monsieur Giraud. The assassin wore gloves. So he must have been sure."

"I do not say it was the assassin himself. It may have been an accomplice who was not aware of that fact."

The magistrate's clerk was gathering up the papers on the table. M. Hautet addressed us:

"Our work here is finished. Perhaps, Monsieur Renauld, you will listen while your evidence is read over to you. I have purposely kept all the proceedings as informal as possible. I have been called original in my methods, but I maintain that there is much to be said for originality. The case is now in the clever hands of the renowned Monsieur Giraud. He will without doubt distinguish himself. Indeed, I wonder that he has not already laid his hands upon the murderers! Madame, again let me assure you of my heartfelt sympathy. Messieurs, I wish you all good day." And, accompanied by his clerk and the commissary, he took his departure.

Poirot tugged out that large turnip of a watch of his and observed the time.

"Let us return to the hotel for lunch, my friend," he said. "And you shall recount to me in full the indiscretions of this morning. No one is observing us. We need make no adieux."

We went quietly out of the room. The examining magistrate had just driven off in his car. I was going down the steps when Poirot's voice arrested me:

"One little moment, my friend." Dexterously he whipped out his yard measure and proceeded, quite solemnly, to measure an overcoat hanging in the hall, from the collar to the hem. I had not seen it hanging there before, and guessed that it belonged to either Mr. Stonor or Jack Renauld.

Then, with a little satisfied grunt, Poirot returned the measure to his pocket and followed me out into the open air.

Twelve

POIROT ELUCIDATES CERTAIN POINTS

"Why did you measure that overcoat?" I asked, with some curiosity, as we walked down the hot white road at a leisurely pace.

"*Parbleu*! to see how long it was," replied my friend imperturbably.

I was vexed. Poirot's incurable habit of making a mystery out of nothing never failed to irritate me. I relapsed into silence, and followed a train of thought of my own. Although I had not noticed them specially at the time, certain words Mrs. Renauld had addressed to her son now recurred to

130

me, fraught with a new significance. "So you did not sail?" she had said, and then had added: *"After all, it does not matter—now."*

What had she meant by that? The words were enigmatical—significant. Was it possible that she knew more than we supposed? She had denied all knowledge of the mysterious mission with which her husband was to have entrusted his son. But was she really less ignorant than she pretended? Could she enlighten us if she chose, and was her silence part of a carefully thought out and preconceived plan?

The more I thought about it, the more I was convinced that I was right. Mrs. Renauld knew more than she chose to tell. In her surprise at seeing her son, she had momentarily betrayed herself. I felt convinced that she knew, if not the assassins, at least the motive for the assassination. But some very powerful considerations must keep her silent.

"You think profoundly, my friend," remarked Poirot, breaking in upon my reflections. "What is it that intrigues you so?"

I told him, sure of my ground, though feeling expectant that he would ridicule my suspicions. But to my surprise he nodded thoughtfully.

"You are quite right, Hastings. From the beginning I have been sure that she was keeping something back. At first I suspected her, if not of inspiring, at least of conniving at the crime."

"You suspected *her?*" I cried.

"But certainly. She benefits enormously—in fact, by this new will, she is the only person to benefit. So, from the start, she was singled out for attention. You may have noticed that I took an early opportunity of examining her wrists. I wished to see whether there was any possibility that she had gagged and bound herself. *Eh bien*, I saw at once that there was no fake, the cords had actually been drawn so tight as to cut into the flesh. That ruled out the possibility of her having committed the crime single-handed. But it was still possible for her to have connived at it, or to have been the instigator with an accomplice. Moreover, the story, as she told it, was singularly familiar to me—the masked men that she could not recognize, the mention of 'the secret'—I had heard, or read, all these things before. Another little detail confirmed my belief that she was not speaking the truth. *The wristwatch, Hastings, the wristwatch!*"

Again that wristwatch! Poirot was eyeing me curiously.

"You see, *mon ami*? You comprehend?"

"No," I replied with some ill humour. "I neither see nor comprehend. You make all these confounded mysteries, and it's useless asking you to explain. You always like keeping something up your sleeve to the last minute."

"Do not enrage yourself, my friend," said

132

Poirot, with a smile. "I will explain if you wish. But not a word to Giraud, *c'est entendu*? He treats me as an old one of no importance! *We shall see!* In common fairness I gave him a hint. If he does not choose to act upon it, that is his own lookout."

I assured Poirot that he could rely upon my discretion.

"*C'est bien!* Let us then employ our little grey cells. Tell me, my friend, at what time, according to you, did the tragedy take place?"

"Why, at two o'clock or thereabouts," I said, astonished. "You remember, Mrs. Renauld told us that she heard the clock strike while the men were in the room."

"Exactly, and on the strength of that, you, the examining magistrate, Bex, and everyone else, accept the time without further question. But I, Hercule Poirot, say that Madame Renauld lied. *The crime took place at least two hours earlier.*"

"But the doctors—"

"They declared, after examination of the body, that death had taken place between ten and seven hours previously. *Mon ami*, for some reason it was imperative that the crime should seem to have taken place later than it actually did. You have read of a smashed watch or clock recording the exact hour of a crime? So that the time should not rest on Madame Renauld's testimony alone, someone moved on the hands of that wristwatch to two o'clock, and then dashed it violently to the ground. But, as is often the case, they defeated their own object. The glass was smashed, but the mechanism of the watch was uninjured. It was a most disastrous manoeuvre on their part, for it at once drew my attention to two points—first, that Madame Renauld was lying; secondly, that there must be some vital reason for the postponement of the time."

"But what reason could there be?"

"Ah, that is the question! There we have the whole mystery. As yet, I cannot explain it. There is only one idea that presents itself to me as having a possible connexion."

"And that is?"

"The last train left Merlinville at seventeen minutes past twelve."

I followed it out slowly.

"So that, the crime apparently taking place some two hours later, anyone leaving by that train would have an unimpeachable alibi!"

"Perfect, Hastings! You have it!"

I sprang up.

"But we must inquire at the station! Surely they cannot have failed to notice two foreigners who left by that train! We must go there at once!"

"You think so, Hastings?"

"Of course. Let us go there now."

Poirot restrained my ardour with a light touch upon the arm.

"Go by all means if you wish, *mon ami*—but if you go, I should not ask for particulars of two foreigners."

I stared and he said rather impatiently:

"*Là, là*, you do not believe all that rigmarole, do you? The masked men and all the rest of *cette histoire-là!*"

His words took me so much aback, that I hardly knew how to respond. He went on serenely:

"You heard me say to Giraud, did you not, that all the details of this crime were familiar to me? *Eh bien*, that presupposes one of two things, either the brain that planned the first crime also planned this one, or else an account read of a *cause célèbre* unconsciously remained in our assassin's memory and prompted the details. I shall be able to pronounce definitely on that after—" He broke off.

I was revolving sundry matters in my mind.

"But Mr. Renauld's letter? It distinctly mentions a secret and Santiago!"

"Undoubtedly there was a secret in Monsieur Renauld's life—there can be no doubt of that. On the other hand, the word Santiago, to my mind, is a red herring, dragged continually across the track to put us off the scent. It is possible that it was used in the same way on Monsieur Renauld, to keep him from directing his suspicions to a quarter nearer at hand. Oh, be assured, Hastings, the danger that threatened him was not in

135

Santiago, it was near at hand, in France."

He spoke so gravely, and with such assurance, that I could not fail to be convinced. But I essayed one final objection:

"And the match and cigarette end found near the body? What of them?"

A light of pure enjoyment lit up Poirot's face.

"Planted! Deliberately planted there for Giraud or one of his tribe to find! Ah, he is smart, Giraud, he can do his tricks! So can a good retriever dog. He comes in so pleased with himself. For hours he has crawled on his stomach. 'See what I have found,' he says. And then again to me: 'What do you see here?' Me, I answer, with profound and deep truth, 'Nothing.' And Giraud, the great Giraud, he laughs, he thinks to himself, 'Oh, he is imbecile, this old one!' *But we shall see. . . .*"

But my mind had reverted to the main facts.

"Then all this story of the masked men—?"

"Is false."

"What really happened?"

Poirot shrugged his shoulders.

"One person could tell us—Madame Renauld. But she will not speak. Threats and entreaties would not move her. A remarkable woman that, Hastings. I recognized as soon as I saw her that I had to deal with a woman of unusual character. At first, as I told you, I was inclined to suspect her of being concerned in the crime. Afterwards I altered my opinion."

"What made you do that?"

"Her spontaneous and genuine grief at the sight of her husband's body. I could swear that the agony in that cry of hers was genuine."

"Yes," I said thoughtfully, "one cannot mistake these things."

"I beg your pardon, my friend—one can always be mistaken. Regard a great actress, does not her acting of grief carry you away and impress you with its reality? No, however strong my own impression and belief, I needed other evidence before I allowed myself to be satisfied. The great criminal can be a great actor. I base my certainty in this case not upon my own impression, but upon the undeniable fact that Madame Renauld actually fainted. I turned up her eyelids and felt her pulse. There was no deception—the swoon was genuine. Therefore I was satisfied that her anguish was real and not assumed. Besides, a small additional point without interest, it was unnecessary for Madame Renauld to exhibit unrestrained grief. She had had one paroxysm on learning of her husband's death, and there would be no need for her to simulate another such a violent one on beholding his body. No, Madame Renauld was not her husband's murderess. But why has she lied? She lied about the wristwatch, she lied about the masked men—she lied about a third thing. Tell me, Hastings, what is your explanation of the open door?"

"Well," I said, rather embarrassed, "I suppose it was an oversight. They forgot to shut it."

Poirot shook his head, and sighed.

"That is the explanation of Giraud. It does not satisfy me. There is a meaning behind that open door which for the moment I cannot fathom. One thing I am fairly sure of—they did not leave through the door. They left by the window."

"What?"

"Precisely."

"But there were no footmarks in the flower bed underneath."

"No—and there ought to have been. Listen, Hastings. The gardener, Auguste, as you heard him say, planted both those beds the preceding afternoon. In the one there are plentiful impressions of his big hobnailed boots—in the other, *none!* You see? Someone had passed that way, someone who, to obliterate their footprints, smoothed over the surface of the bed with a rake."

"Where did they get a rake?"

"Where they got the spade and the gardening gloves," said Poirot impatiently. "There is no difficulty about that."

"What makes you think that they left that way, though? Surely it is more probable that they entered by the window, and left by the door?"

"That is possible, of course. Yet I have a strong idea that they left by the window."

"I think you are wrong."

138

"Perhaps, *mon ami*."

I mused, thinking over the new field of conjecture that Poirot's deductions had opened up to me. I recalled my wonder at his cryptic allusion to the flower bed and the wristwatch. His remarks had seemed so meaningless at the moment, and now, for the first time, I realized how remarkably, from a few slight incidents, he had unravelled much of the mystery that surrounded the case. I paid a belated homage to my friend.

"In the meantime," I said, considering, "although we know a great deal more than we did, we are no nearer to solving the mystery of who killed Mr. Renauld."

"No," said Poirot cheerfully. "In fact we are a great deal farther off."

The fact seemed to afford him such peculiar satisfaction that I gazed at him in wonder. He met my eye and smiled.

Suddenly a light burst upon me.

"Poirot! Mrs. Renauld! I see it now. She must be shielding somebody."

From the quietness with which Poirot received my remark, I could see that the idea had already occurred to him.

"Yes," he said thoughtfully. "Shielding some-one—or screening someone. One of the two."

Then, as we entered our hotel, he enjoined silence on me with a gesture.

Thirteen

THE GIRL WITH THE ANXIOUS EYES

We lunched with an excellent appetite. For a while we ate in silence, and then Poirot observed maliciously: "*Eh bien*! And your indiscretions! You recount them not?"

I felt myself blushing.

"Oh, you mean this morning?" I endeavoured to adopt a tone of absolute nonchalance.

But I was no match for Poirot. In a very few minutes he had extracted the whole story from me, his eyes twinkling as he did so.

"*Tiens*! A story of the most romantic. What is her name, this charming young lady?"

I had to confess that I did not know.

"Still more romantic! The first *rencontre* in the train from Paris, the second here. Journeys end in lovers' meetings, is not that the saying?"

"Don't be an ass, Poirot."

"Yesterday it was Mademoiselle Daubreuil, today it is Mademoiselle—Cinderella! Decidedly you have the heart of a Turk, Hastings! You should establish a harem!"

"It's all very well to rag me. Mademoiselle Daubreuil is a very beautiful girl, and I do admire her immensely—I don't mind admitting it. The other's nothing—I don't suppose I shall ever see her again."

"You do not propose to see the lady again?"

His last words were almost a question, and I was aware of the sharpness with which he darted a glance at me. And before my eyes, writ large in letters of fire, I saw the words "Hôtel du Phare," and I heard again her voice saying, "Come and look me up," and my own answering with *empressement* "I will."

I answered Poirot lightly enough:

"She asked me to look her up, but, of course, I shan't."

"Why 'of course'?"

"Well, I don't want to."

"Mademoiselle Cinderella is staying at the Hôtel d'Angleterre you told me, did you not?"

"No. Hôtel du Phare."

"True, I forgot."

A moment's misgiving shot across my mind. Surely I had never mentioned any hotel to Poirot. I looked across at him and felt reassured. He was cutting his bread into neat little squares, completely absorbed in his task. He must have fancied I had told him where the girl was staying.

We had coffee outside facing the sea. Poirot smoked one of his tiny cigarettes, and then drew his watch from his pocket.

"The train to Paris leaves at 2:25," he observed. "I should be starting."

"Paris?" I cried.

"That is what I said, *mon ami*."

"You are going to Paris? But why?"

He replied very seriously:

"To look for the murderer of Monsieur Renauld."

"You think he is in Paris?"

"I am quite certain that he is not. Nevertheless, it is there that I must look for him. You do not understand, but I will explain it all to you in good time. Believe me, this journey to Paris is necessary. I shall not be away long. In all probability I shall return tomorrow. I do not propose that you should accompany me. Remain here and keep an eye on Giraud. Also cultivate the society of Monsieur Renauld *fils*."

"That reminds me," I said. "I meant to ask you how you knew about those two?"

"*Mon ami*—I know human nature. Throw together a boy like young Renauld and a beautiful girl like Mademoiselle Marthe and the result is almost inevitable. Then, the quarrel! It was money, or a woman, and, remembering Léonie's description of the lad's anger, I decided on the latter. So I made my guess—and I was right."

"You already suspected that she loved young Renauld?" Poirot smiled.

"At any rate, *I saw that she had anxious eyes*. That is how I always think of Mademoiselle Daubreuil—*as the girl with the anxious eyes*."

His voice was so grave that it impressed me uncomfortably.

"What do you mean by that, Poirot?"

"I fancy, my friend, that we shall see before very long. But I must start."

"I will come and see you off," I said, rising.

"You will do nothing of the sort. I forbid it."

He was so peremptory that I stared at him in surprise. He nodded emphatically.

"I mean it, *mon ami*. Au revoir."

I felt rather at a loose end after Poirot had left me. I strolled down to the beach and watched the bathers, without feeling energetic enough to join them. I rather fancied that Cinderella might be disporting herself among them in some wonderful costume, but I saw no signs of her. I strolled aimlessly along the sands towards the farther end of the town. It occurred to me that, after all, it would only be decent feeling on my part to inquire after the girl. And it would save trouble in the end. The matter would then be finished with. There would be no need for me to trouble about her any further. But if I did not go at all, she might quite possibly come and look me up at the villa.

Accordingly, I left the beach, and walked inland. I soon found the Hôtel du Phare, a very unpretentious building. It was annoying in the extreme not to know the lady's name and, to save my dignity, I decided to stroll inside and look around. Probably I should find her in the lounge. I went in, but there was no sign of her. I waited for some time, till my impatience got the better of me. I took the concierge aside and slipped five francs into his hand.

"I wish to see a lady who is staying here. A young English lady, small and dark. I am not sure of her name."

The man shook his head and seemed to be suppressing a grin.

"There is no such lady as you describe staying here."

"But the lady told me she was staying here."

"Monsieur must have made a mistake—or it is more likely the lady did, since there has been another gentleman here inquiring for her."

"What is that you say?" I cried, surprised.

"But yes, monsieur. A gentleman who described her just as you have done."

"What was he like?"

"He was a small gentleman, well dressed, very neat, very spotless, the moustache very stiff, the head of a peculiar shape, and the eyes green."

Poirot! So that was why he refused to let me accompany him to the station. The impertinence of it! I would thank him not to meddle in my concerns. Did he fancy I needed a nurse to look after me?

Thanking the man, I departed, somewhat at a

loss, and still much incensed with my meddle-some friend.

But where was the lady? I set aside my wrath and tried to puzzle it out. Evidently, through inadvertence, she had named the wrong hotel. Then another thought struck me. Was it inadvertence? Or had she deliberately withheld her name and given me the wrong address?

The more I thought about it, the more I felt convinced that this last surmise of mine was right. For some reason or other she did not wish to let the acquaintance ripen into friendship. And, though half an hour earlier this had been precisely my own view, I did not enjoy having the tables turned upon me. The whole affair was profoundly unsatisfactory, and I went up to the Villa Geneviève in a condition of distinct ill humour. I did not go to the house, but went up the path to the little bench by the shed, and sat there moodily enough.

I was distracted from my thoughts by the sound of voices close at hand. In a second or two I realized that they came, not from the garden I was in, but from the adjoining garden of the Villa Marguerite, and that they were approaching rapidly. A girl's voice was speaking, a voice that I recognized as that of the beautiful Marthe.

"*Chéri*," she was saying, "is it really true? Are all our troubles over?"

"You know it, Marthe," Jack Renauld replied.

"Nothing can part us now, beloved. The last obstacle to our union is removed. Nothing can take you from me."

"Nothing?" the girl murmured. "Oh Jack, Jack—I am afraid."

I had moved to depart, realizing that I was quite unintentionally eavesdropping. As I rose to my feet, I caught sight of them through a gap in the hedge. They stood together facing me, the man's arm round the girl, his eyes looking into hers. They were a splendid-looking couple, the dark, well-knit boy, and the fair young goddess. They seemed made for each other as they stood there, happy in spite of the terrible tragedy that overshadowed their young lives.

But the girl's face was troubled, and Jack Renauld seemed to recognize it, as he held her closer to him and asked:

"But what are you afraid of, darling? What is there to fear—now?"

And then I saw the look in her eyes, the look Poirot had spoken of, as she murmured, so that I almost guessed at the words:

"I am afraid—for *you*."

I did not hear young Renauld's answer, for my attention was distracted by an unusual appearance a little farther down the hedge. There appeared to be a brown bush there, which seemed odd, to say the least of it, so early in the summer. I stepped along to investigate, but, at my advance, the brown bush withdrew itself precipitately, and faced me with a finger to its lips. It was Giraud.

Enjoining caution, he led the way round the shed until we were out of ear-shot.

"What were you doing there?" I asked.

"Exactly what you were doing—listening."

"But I was not there on purpose!"

"Ah!" said Giraud. "I was."

As always, I admired the man while disliking him. He looked me up and down with a sort of contemptuous disfavour.

"You didn't help matters by butting in. I might have heard something useful in a minute. What have you done with your old fossil?"

"Monsieur Poirot has gone to Paris," I replied coldly.

Giraud snapped his fingers disdainfully. "So he has gone to Paris, has he? Well, a good thing. The longer he stays there the better. But what does he think he will find there?"

I thought I read in the question a tinge of uneasiness. I drew myself up.

"That I am not at liberty to say," I said quietly.

Giraud subjected me to a piercing stare.

"He has probably enough sense not to tell *you*," he remarked rudely. "Good afternoon. I'm busy." And with that he turned on his heel, and left me without ceremony.

Matters seemed at a standstill at the Villa Geneviève. Giraud evidently did not desire my company and, from what I had seen, it seemed fairly certain that Jack Renauld did not either.

I went back to the town, had an enjoyable bathe, and returned to the hotel. I turned in early, wondering whether the following day would bring forth anything of interest.

I was wholly unprepared for what it did bring forth. I was eating my *petit déjeuner* in the dining room, when the waiter, who had been talking to someone outside, came back in obvious excitement. He hesitated for a minute, fidgeting with his napkin, and then burst out:

"Monsieur will pardon me, but he is connected, is he not, with the affair at the Villa Geneviève?"

"Yes," I said eagerly. "Why?"

"Monsieur has not heard the news, though?"

"What news?"

"That there has been another murder there last night!"

"What?"

Leaving my breakfast, I caught up my hat and ran as fast as I could. Another murder—and Poirot away! What fatality. But who had been murdered?

I dashed in at the gate. A group of servants were in the drive, talking and gesticulating. I caught hold of Françoise.

"What has happened?"

"Oh, monsieur! monsieur! Another death! It is terrible. There is a curse upon the house. But yes,

I say it, a curse! They should send for Monsieur le Curé to bring some holy water. Never will I sleep another night under that roof. It might be my turn, who knows?"

She crossed herself.

"Yes," I cried, "but who has been killed?"

"Do I know—me? A man—a stranger. They found him up there—in the shed—not a hundred yards from where they found poor Monsieur. And that is not all. He is stabbed—stabbed to the heart *with the same dagger!*"

Fourteen

THE SECOND BODY

Waiting for no more, I turned and ran up the path to the shed. The two men on guard there stood aside to let me pass and, filled with excitement, I entered.

The light was dim, the place was a mere rough wooden erection to keep old pots and tools in. I had entered impetuously, but on the threshold I checked myself, fascinated by the spectacle before me.

Giraud was on his hands and knees, a pocket torch in his hand with which he was examining every inch of the ground. He looked up with a frown at my entrance, then his face relaxed a little in a sort of good-humoured contempt.

"There he is," said Giraud, flashing his torch to the far corner.

I stepped across.

The dead man lay straight upon his back. He was of medium height, swarthy of complexion, and possibly about fifty years of age. He was neatly dressed in a dark blue suit, well cut, and probably made by an expensive tailor, but not new. His face was terribly convulsed, and on his left side, just over the heart, the hilt of a dagger stood up, black and shining. I recognized it. It was the same dagger I had seen reposing in the glass jar the preceding morning!

"I'm expecting the doctor any minute," explained Giraud. "Although we hardly need him. There's no doubt what the man died of. He was stabbed to the heart, and death must have been pretty well instantaneous."

"When was it done? Last night?"

Giraud shook his head.

"Hardly. I don't lay down the law on medical evidence, but the man's been dead well over twelve hours. When do you say you last saw that dagger?"

"About ten o'clock yesterday morning."

"Then I should be inclined to fix the crime as being done not long after that."

"But people were passing and repassing this shed continually."

Giraud laughed disagreeably.

"You progress to a marvel! Who told you he was killed in this shed?"

"Well—" I felt flustered. "I—I assumed it."

"Oh, what a fine detective! Look at him. Does a man stabbed to the heart fall like that—neatly with his feet together, and his arms to his sides? No. Again, does a man lie down on his back and permit himself to be stabbed without raising a hand to defend himself? It is absurd, is it not? But see here—and here—" He flashed the torch along the ground. I saw curious irregular marks in the soft dirt. "He was dragged here after he was dead. Half dragged, half carried by two people. Their tracks do not show on the hard ground outside, and here they have been careful to obliterate them; but one of the two was a woman, my young friend."

"A woman?"

"Yes."

"But if the tracks are obliterated, how do you know?"

"Because, blurred as they are, the prints of the woman's shoe are unmistakable. Also, by *this*." And, leaning forward, he drew something from the handle of the dagger and held it up for me to see. It was a woman's long black hair, similar to the one Poirot had taken from the armchair in the library.

With a slightly ironic smile he wound it round the dagger again.

"We will leave things as they are as much as possible," he explained. "It pleases the examining magistrate. Well, do you notice anything else?"

I was forced to shake my head.

"Look at his hands."

I did. The nails were broken and discoloured and the skin was hard. It hardly enlightened me as much as I should have liked it to have done. I looked up at Giraud.

"They are not the hands of a gentleman," he said, answering my look. "On the contrary, his clothes are those of a well-to-do man. That is curious, is it not?"

"Very curious," I agreed.

"And none of his clothing is marked. What do we learn from that? This man was trying to pass himself off as other than he was. He was masquerading. Why? Did he fear something? Was he trying to escape by disguising himself? As yet we do not know, but one thing we do know—he was as anxious to conceal his identity as we are to discover it."

He looked down at the body again.

"As before, there are no fingerprints on the handle of the dagger. The murderer again wore gloves."

"You think, then, that the murderer was the same in both cases?" I asked eagerly.

Giraud became inscrutable.

"Never mind what I think. We shall see. Marchaud!"

The *sergent de ville* appeared at the door.

"Monsieur?"

"Why is Madame Renauld not here? I sent for her a quarter of an hour ago."

"She is coming up the path now, monsieur, and her son with her."

"Good. I only want one at a time, though."

Marchaud saluted and disappeared again. A moment later he reappeared with Mrs. Renauld.

"Here is Madame."

Giraud came forward with a curt bow.

"This way, madame." He led her across, and then, standing suddenly aside, "Here is the man. Do you know him?"

And as he spoke, his eyes, gimlet-like, bored into her face, seeking to read her mind, noting every indication of her manner.

But Mrs. Renauld remained perfectly calm—too calm, I felt. She looked down at the corpse almost without interest, certainly without any sign of agitation or recognition.

"No," she said. "I have never seen him in my life. He is quite a stranger to me."

"You are sure?"

"Quite sure."

"You do not recognize in him one of your assailants, for instance?"

"No." She seemed to hesitate, as though struck by the idea. "No, I do not think so. Of course they wore beards—false ones the examining magistrate thought—but still, no." Now she seemed to make her mind up definitely. "I am sure neither of the two was this man."

"Very well, madame. That is all, then."

She stepped out with head erect, the sun flashing on the silver threads in her hair. Jack Renauld succeeded her. He, too, failed to identify the man in a completely natural manner.

Giraud merely grunted. Whether he was pleased or chagrined I could not tell. He called to Marchaud.

"You have got the other there?"

"Yes, monsieur."

"Bring her in, then."

"The other" was Madame Daubreuil. She came indignantly, protesting with vehemence.

"I object, monsieur! This is an outrage! What have I to do with all this?"

"Madame," said Giraud brutally, "I am investigating not one murder, but two murders! For all I know you may have committed them both."

"How dare you?" she cried. "How dare you insult me by such a wild accusation! It is infamous!"

"Infamous, is it? What about this?" Stooping, he again detached the hair, and held it up. "Do you see this, madame?" He advanced towards her. "You permit that I see whether it matches?"

With a cry she started backwards, white to the lips.

"It is false, I swear it. I know nothing of the crime—of either crime. Anyone who says I do lies! Ah, *mon Dieu*, what shall I do?"

"Calm yourself, madame," said Giraud coldly. "No one has accused you as yet. But you will do well to answer my questions without more ado."

"Anything you wish, monsieur."

"Look at the dead man. Have you ever seen him before?"

Drawing nearer, a little of the colour creeping back to her face, Madame Daubreuil looked down at the victim with a certain amount of interest and curiosity. Then she shook her head.

"I do not know him."

It seemed impossible to doubt her, the words came so naturally. Giraud dismissed her with a nod of the head.

"You are letting her go?" I asked in a low voice. "Is that wise? Surely that black hair is from her head."

"I do not need teaching my business," said Giraud dryly. "She is under surveillance. I have no wish to arrest her as yet."

Then, frowning, he gazed down at the body.

"Should you say that was a Spanish type at all?" he asked suddenly.

I considered the face carefully.

"No," I said at last. "I should put him down as a Frenchman most decidedly."

Giraud gave a grunt of dissatisfaction.

"Same here."

He stood there for a moment, then with an imperative gesture he waved me aside, and once more, on hands and knees, he continued his search of the floor of the shed. He was marvellous. Nothing escaped him. Inch by inch he went over the floor, turning over pots, examining old sacks. He pounced on a bundle by the door, but it proved to be only a ragged coat and trousers, and he flung it down again with a snarl. Two pairs of old gloves interested him, but in the end he shook his head and laid them aside. Then he went back to the pots, methodically turning them over one by one. In the end he rose to his feet, and shook his head thoughtfully. He seemed baffled and perplexed. I think he had forgotten my presence.

But at that moment a stir and bustle was heard outside, and our old friend, the examining magistrate, accompanied by his clerk and M. Bex, with the doctor behind them, came bustling in.

"But this is extraordinary, Monsieur Giraud," cried M. Hautet. "Another crime! Ah, we have not got to the bottom of this case. There is some deep mystery here. But who is the victim this time?"

"That is just what nobody can tell us, monsieur. He has not been identified."

"Where is the body?" asked the doctor.

Giraud moved aside a little.

"There in the corner. He has been stabbed to the heart, as you see. And with the dagger that was stolen yesterday morning. I fancy that the murder followed hard upon the theft—but that is for you to say. You can handle the dagger freely—there are no fingerprints on it."

The doctor knelt down by the dead man, and Giraud turned to the examining magistrate.

"A pretty little problem, is it not? But I shall solve it."

"And so no one can identify him," mused the magistrate. "Could it possibly be one of the assassins? They may have fallen out among themselves."

Giraud shook his head.

"The man is a Frenchman—I would take my oath on that—"

But at that moment they were interrupted by the doctor, who was sitting back on his heels with a perplexed expression.

"You say he was killed yesterday morning?"

"I fix it by the theft of the dagger," explained Giraud. "He may, of course, have been killed later in the day."

"Later in the day? Fiddlesticks! This man has been dead at least forty-eight hours, and probably longer."

We stared at each other in blank amazement.

Fifteen

A Photograph

The doctor's words were so surprising that we were all momentarily taken aback. Here was a man stabbed with a dagger which we knew to have been stolen only twenty-four hours previously, and yet Dr. Durand asserted positively that he had been dead at least forty-eight hours! The whole thing was fantastic to the last extreme.

We were still recovering from the surprise of the doctor's announcement, when a telegram was brought to me. It had been sent up from the hotel to the villa. I tore it open. It was from Poirot, and announced his return by the train arriving at Merlinville at 12:28.

I looked at my watch and saw that I had just time to get comfortably to the station and meet him there. I felt that it was of the utmost importance that he should know at once of the new and startling developments in the case.

Evidently, I reflected, Poirot had had no difficulty in finding what he wanted in Paris. The quickness of his return proved that. Very few hours had sufficed. I wondered how he would take the exciting news I had to impart.

The train was some minutes late, and I strolled

aimlessly up and down the platform, until it occurred to me that I might pass the time by asking a few questions as to who had left Merlinville by the last train on the evening of the tragedy.

I approached the chief porter, an intelligent-looking man, and had little difficulty in persuading him to enter upon the subject. It was a disgrace to the police, he hotly affirmed, that such brigands or assassins should be allowed to go about unpunished. I hinted that there was some possibility they might have left by the midnight train, but he negatived the idea decidedly. He would have noticed two foreigners—he was sure of it. Only about twenty people had left by the train, and he could not have failed to observe them.

I do not know what put the idea into my head— possibly it was the deep anxiety underlying Marthe Daubreuil's tones—but I asked suddenly:

"Young Monsieur Renauld—he did not leave by that train, did he?"

"Ah, no, monsieur. To arrive and start off again within half an hour, it would not be amusing, that!"

I stared at the man, the significance of his words almost escaping me. Then I saw.

"You mean," I said, my heart beating a little, "that Monsieur Jack Renauld arrived at Merlinville that evening?"

"But yes, monsieur. By the last train arriving the other way, the 11:40."

My brain whirled. That, then, was the reason of Marthe's poignant anxiety. Jack Renauld had been in Merlinville on the night of the crime. But why had he not said so? Why, on the contrary, had he led us to believe that he had remained in Cherbourg? Remembering his frank boyish countenance, I could hardly bring myself to believe that he had any connexion with the crime. Yet why this silence on his part about so vital a matter? One thing was certain, Marthe had known all along. Hence her anxiety, and her eager questioning of Poirot as to whether anyone was suspected.

My cogitations were interrupted by the arrival of the train, and in another moment I was greeting Poirot. The little man was radiant. He beamed and vociferated and, forgetting my English reluctance, embraced me warmly on the platform.

"*Mon cher ami*, I have succeeded—but succeeded to a marvel!"

"Indeed? I'm delighted to hear it. Have you heard the latest here?"

"How would you that I should hear anything? There have been some developments, eh? The brave Giraud, he has made an arrest? Or even arrests, perhaps? Ah, but I will make him look foolish, that one! But where are you taking me, my friend? Do we not go to the hotel? It is necessary that I attend to my moustaches—they are deplorably limp from the heat of travelling. Also, without doubt, there is dust on my coat. And my tie, that I must rearrange."

I cut short his remonstrances.

"My dear Poirot—never mind all that. We must go to the villa at once. *There has been another murder!*"

Never have I seen a man so flabbergasted. His jaw dropped. All the jauntiness went out of his bearing. He stared at me openmouthed.

"What is that you say? Another murder? Ah, then, but I am all wrong. I have failed. Giraud may mock himself at me—he will have reason!"

"You did not expect it, then?"

"I? Not the least in the world. It demolishes my theory—it ruins everything—it—Ah, no!" He stopped dead, thumping himself on the chest. "It is impossible. I *cannot* be wrong! The facts, taken methodically, and in their proper order, admit of only one explanation. I must be right! I *am* right!"

"But then—"

He interrupted me.

"Wait, my friend. I must be right, therefore this new murder is impossible unless—unless—Oh, wait, I implore you. Say no word."

He was silent for a moment or two, then resuming his normal manner, he said in a quiet assured voice:

"The victim is a man of middle age. His body

was found in the locked shed near the scene of the crime and had been dead at least forty-eight hours. And it is most probable that he was stabbed in a similar manner to Mr. Renauld, though not necessarily in the back."

It was my turn to gape—and gape I did. In all my knowledge of Poirot he had never done anything so amazing as this. And, almost inevitably, a doubt crossed my mind.

"Poirot," I cried, "you're pulling my leg. You've heard all about it already."

He turned his earnest gaze upon me reproachfully.

"Would I do such a thing? I assure you that I have heard nothing whatsoever. Did you not observe the shock your news was to me?"

"But how on earth could you know all that?"

"I was right, then? But I knew it. The little grey cells, my friend, the little grey cells! They told me. Thus, and in no other way, could there have been a second death. Now tell me all. If we go round to the left here, we can take a short cut across the golf links which will bring us to the back of the Villa Geneviève much more quickly."

As we walked, taking the way he had indicated, I recounted all I knew. Poirot listened attentively.

"The dagger was in the wound, you say? That is curious. You are sure it was the same one?"

"Absolutely certain. That's what makes it so impossible."

"Nothing is impossible. There may have been two daggers."

I raised my eyebrows.

"Surely that is in the highest degree unlikely? It would be a most extraordinary coincidence."

"You speak as usual, without reflection, Hastings. In some cases two identical weapons *would* be highly improbable. But not here. This particular weapon was a war souvenir which was made to Jack Renauld's orders. It is really highly unlikely, when you come to think of it, that he should have had only one made. Very probably he would have another for his own use."

"But nobody has mentioned such a thing," I objected.

A hint of the lecturer crept into Poirot's tone.

"My friend, in working upon a case, one does not take into account only the things that are 'mentioned.' There is no reason to mention many things which may be important. Equally, there is often an excellent reason for *not* mentioning them. You can take your choice of the two motives."

I was silent, impressed in spite of myself. Another few minutes brought us to the famous shed. We found all our friends there, and after an interchange of polite amenities, Poirot began his task.

Having watched Giraud at work, I was keenly interested. Poirot bestowed but a cursory glance on the surroundings. The only thing he examined was the ragged coat and trousers by the door. A disdainful smile rose to Giraud's lips, and, as though noting it, Poirot flung the bundle down again.

"Old clothes of the gardener's?" he queried.

"Exactly," said Giraud.

Poirot knelt down by the body. His fingers were rapid but methodical. He examined the texture of the clothes, and satisfied himself that there were no marks on them. The boots he subjected to special care, also the dirty and broken fingernails. While examining the latter he threw a quick question at Giraud.

"You saw them?"

"Yes, I saw them," replied the other. His face remained inscrutable.

Suddenly Poirot stiffened.

"Dr. Durand!"

"Yes?" The doctor came forward.

"There is foam on the lips. You observed it?"

"I didn't notice it, I must admit."

"But you observe it now?"

"Oh, certainly."

Poirot again shot a question at Giraud.

"You noticed it without doubt?"

The other did not reply. Poirot proceeded. The dagger had been withdrawn from the wound. It reposed in a glass jar by the side of the body. Poirot examined it, then he studied the wound closely. When he looked up, his eyes were excited and shone with the green light I knew so well.

"It is a strange wound, this! It has not bled. There is no stain on the clothes. The blade of the dagger is slightly discoloured, that is all. What do you think, *monsieur le docteur?*"

"I can only say that it is most abnormal."

"It is not abnormal at all. It is most simple. The man was stabbed *after he was dead.*" And, stilling the clamour of voices that arose with a wave of his hand, Poirot turned to Giraud and added: "M. Giraud agrees with me, do you not, monsieur?"

Whatever Giraud's real belief, he accepted the position without moving a muscle. Calmly and almost scornfully he replied:

"Certainly I agree."

The murmur of surprise and interest broke out again.

"But what an idea!" cried M. Hautet. "To stab a man after he is dead! Barbaric! Unheard of! Some unappeasable hate perhaps."

"No," said Poirot. "I should fancy it was done quite cold-bloodedly—to create an impression."

"What impression?"

"The impression it nearly did create," returned Poirot oracularly.

M. Bex had been thinking.

"How, then, was the man killed?"

165

"He was not killed. He died. He died, if I am not much mistaken, of an epileptic fit!"

This statement of Poirot's again aroused considerable excitement. Dr. Durand knelt down again, and made a searching examination. At last he rose to his feet.

"Monsieur Poirot, I am inclined to believe that you are correct in your assertion. I was misled to begin with. The incontrovertible fact that the man had been stabbed distracted my attention from any other indications."

Poirot was the hero of the hour. The examining magistrate was profuse in compliments. Poirot responded gracefully, and then excused himself on the pretext that neither he nor I had yet lunched, and that he wished to repair the ravages of the journey. As we were about to leave the shed, Giraud approached us.

"One other thing, Monsieur Poirot," he said, in his suave mocking voice. "We found this coiled round the handle of the dagger—a woman's hair."

"Ah!" said Poirot. "A woman's hair? What woman's, I wonder?"

"I wonder also," said Giraud. Then, with a bow, he left us.

"He was insistent, the good Giraud," said Poirot thoughtfully, as we walked towards the hotel. "I wonder in what direction he hopes to mislead me? A woman's hair—h'm!"

We lunched heartily, but I found Poirot

somewhat distrait and inattentive. Afterwards we went up to our sitting room, and there I begged him to tell me something of his mysterious journey to Paris.

"Willingly, my friend. I went to Paris to find *this*."

He took from his pocket a small faded newspaper cutting. It was the reproduction of a woman's photograph. He handed it to me. I uttered an exclamation.

"You recognize it, my friend?"

I nodded. Although the photo obviously dated from very many years back, and the hair was dressed in a different style, the likeness was unmistakable.

"Madame Daubreuil!" I exclaimed.

Poirot shook his head with a smile.

"Not quite correct, my friend. She did not call herself by that name in those days. That is a picture of the notorious Madame Beroldy!"

Madame Beroldy! In a flash the whole thing came back to me. The murder trial that had evoked such worldwide interest.

The Beroldy Case.

Sixteen

THE BEROLDY CASE

Some twenty years or so before the opening of the present story, Monsieur Arnold Beroldy, a native of Lyons, arrived in Paris accompanied by his pretty wife and their little daughter, a mere babe. Monsieur Beroldy was a junior partner in a firm of wine merchants, a stout middle-aged man, fond of the good things of life, devoted to his charming wife, and altogether unremarkable in every way. The firm in which Monsieur Beroldy was a partner was a small one and, although doing well, it did not yield a large income to the junior partner. The Beroldys had a small apartment and lived in a very modest fashion to begin with.

But, unremarkable though Monsieur Beroldy might be, his wife was plentifully gilded with the brush of Romance. Young and good-looking, and gifted withal with a singular charm of manner, Madame Beroldy at once created a stir in the quarter, especially when it began to be whispered that some interesting mystery surrounded her birth. It was rumoured that she was the illegitimate daughter of a Russian Grand Duke. Others asserted that it was an Austrian Archduke, and that the union was legal, though morganatic. But all stories agreed upon one point, that Jeanne Beroldy was the centre of an interesting mystery.

Among the friends and acquaintances of the Beroldys was a young lawyer, Georges Conneau. It was soon evident that the fascinating Jeanne had completely enslaved his heart. Madame Beroldy encouraged the young man in a discreet fashion, but always being careful to affirm her complete devotion to her middle-aged husband. Nevertheless, many spiteful persons did not hesitate to declare that young Conneau was her lover—and not the only one!

When the Beroldys had been in Paris about three months, another personage came upon the scene. This was Mr. Hiram P. Trapp, a native of the United States, and extremely wealthy. Introduced to the charming and mysterious Madame Beroldy, he fell a prompt victim to her fascinations. His admiration was obvious, though strictly respectful.

About this time, Madame Beroldy became more outspoken in her confidences. To several friends, she declared herself greatly worried on her husband's behalf. She explained that he had been drawn into several schemes of a political nature, and also referred to some important papers that had been entrusted to him for safe-keeping and which concerned a "secret" of far-reaching European importance. They had been entrusted to his custody to throw pursuers off the track, but Madame Beroldy was nervous, having recognized several important members of the Revolutionary Circle in Paris.

On the 28th day of November the blow fell. The woman who came daily to clean and cook for the Beroldys was surprised to find the door of the apartment standing wide open. Hearing faint moans issuing from the bedroom, she went in. A terrible sight met her eyes. Madame Beroldy lay on the floor bound hand and foot, uttering feeble moans, having managed to free her mouth from a gag. On the bed was Monsieur Beroldy, lying in a pool of blood, with a knife driven through his heart.

Madame Beroldy's story was clear enough. Suddenly awakened from sleep, she had discerned two masked men bending over her. Stifling her cries, they had bound and gagged her. They had then demanded of Monsieur Beroldy the famous "secret."

But the intrepid wine merchant refused point-blank to accede to their request. Angered by his refusal, one of the men incontinently stabbed him through the heart. With the dead man's keys, they had opened the safe in the corner, and had carried away with them a mass of papers. Both men were heavily bearded, and had worn masks, but Madame Beroldy declared positively that they were Russians.

The affair created an immense sensation. Time went on, and the mysterious bearded men were never traced. And then, just as public interest was beginning to die down, a startling development occurred: Madame Beroldy was arrested and charged with the murder of her husband.

The trial, when it came on, aroused widespread interest. The youth and beauty of the accused, and her mysterious history, were sufficient to make of it a *cause célèbre*.

It was proved beyond doubt that Jeanne Beroldy's parents were a highly respectable and prosaic couple, fruit merchants, who lived on the outskirts of Lyons. The Russian Grand Duke, the court intrigues, and the political schemes—all the stories current were traced back to the lady herself! Remorselessly, the whole story of her life was laid bare. The motive for the murder was found in Mr. Hiram P. Trapp. Mr. Trapp did his best, but, relentlessly and agilely cross-questioned, he was forced to admit that he loved the lady, and that, had she been free, he would have asked her to be his wife. The fact that the relations between them were admittedly platonic strengthened the case against the accused. Debarred from becoming his mistress by the simple honourable nature of the man, Jeanne Beroldy had conceived the monstrous project of ridding herself of her elderly, undistinguished husband and becoming the wife of the rich American.

Throughout, Madame Beroldy confronted her accusers with complete sangfroid and self-possession. Her story never varied. She continued to declare strenuously that she was of royal birth and that she had been substituted for the daughter of the fruit seller at an early age. Absurd and completely unsubstantiated as these statements were, a great number of people believed implicitly in their truth.

But the prosecution was implacable. It denounced the masked "Russians" as a myth, and asserted that the crime had been committed by Madame Beroldy and her lover, Georges Conneau. A warrant was issued for the arrest of the latter, but he had wisely disappeared. Evidence showed that the bonds which secured Madame Beroldy were so loose that she could easily have freed herself.

And then, towards the close of the trial, a letter, posted in Paris, was sent to the Public Prosecutor. It was from Georges Conneau and, without revealing his whereabouts, it contained a full confession of the crime. He declared that he had indeed struck the fatal blow at Madame Beroldy's instigation. The crime had been planned between them. Believing that her husband ill-treated her, and maddened by his own passion for her, a passion which he believed her to return, he had planned the crime and struck the fatal blow that should free the woman he loved from a hateful bondage. Now, for the first time, he learnt of Mr. Hiram P. Trapp, and realized that the woman he loved had betrayed him! Not for his sake did she wish to be free, but in order to marry the wealthy American. She had used him as a cat's paw, and now, in his jealous rage, he turned and denounced her, declaring that throughout he had acted at her instigation.

And then Madame Beroldy proved herself the remarkable woman she undoubtedly was. Without hesitation, she dropped her previous defence, and admitted that the "Russians" were a pure invention on her part. The real murderer was Georges Conneau. Maddened by passion, he had committed the crime, vowing that if she did not keep silence he would exact a terrible vengeance from her. Terrified by his threats, she had consented—also fearing it likely that if she told the truth she might be accused of conniving at the crime. But she had steadfastly refused to have anything more to do with her husband's murderer, and it was in revenge for this attitude on her part that he had written this letter accusing her. She swore solemnly that she had had nothing to do with the planning of the crime, that she had awoke on that memorable night to find Georges Conneau standing over her, the bloodstained knife in his hand.

It was a touch-and-go affair. Madame Beroldy's story was hardly credible. But her address to the jury was a masterpiece. The tears streaming down her face, she spoke of her child, of her woman's honour—of her desire to keep her reputation untarnished for the child's sake. She admitted that, Georges Conneau having been her lover, she might perhaps be held morally responsible for the crime—but, before God, nothing more! She knew that she had committed a grave fault in not denouncing Conneau to the law, but she declared in a broken voice that that was a thing no woman could have done. She had loved him! Could she let her hand be the one to send him to the guillotine? She had been guilty of much, but she was innocent of the terrible crime imputed to her.

However that may have been, her eloquence and personality won the day. Madame Beroldy, amidst a scene of unparalleled excitement, was acquitted.

Despite the utmost endeavours of the police, Georges Conneau was never traced. As for Madame Beroldy, nothing more was heard of her. Taking the child with her, she left Paris to begin a new life.

Seventeen

WE MAKE FURTHER INVESTIGATIONS

I have set down the Beroldy case in full. Of course all the details did not present themselves to my memory as I have recounted them here. Nevertheless, I recalled the case fairly accurately. It had attracted a great deal of interest at the time, and had been fully reported by the English papers, so that it did not need much effort of memory on my part to recollect the salient details.

Just for the moment, in my excitement, it seemed to clear up the whole matter. I admit that I am impulsive, and Poirot deplores my custom of jumping to conclusions, but I think I had some excuse in this instance. The remarkable way in which this discovery justified Poirot's point of view struck me at once.

"Poirot," I said, "I congratulate you. I see everything now."

Poirot lit one of his little cigarettes with his usual precision. Then he looked up.

"And since you see everything now, *mon ami*, what exactly is it that you see?"

"Why, that it was Madame Daubreuil— Beroldy—who murdered Mr. Renauld. The similarity of the two cases proves that beyond a doubt."

"Then you consider that Madame Beroldy was wrongly acquitted? That in actual fact she was guilty of connivance in her husband's murder?"

I opened my eyes wide.

"Of course! Don't you?"

Poirot walked to the end of the room, absentmindedly straightened a chair, and then said thoughtfully:

"Yes, that is my opinion. But there is no 'of course' about it, my friend. Technically speaking, Madame Beroldy is innocent."

"Of that crime, perhaps. But not of this."

Poirot sat down again, and regarded me, his thoughtful air more marked than ever.

"So it is definitely your opinion, Hastings, that Madame Daubreuil murdered Monsieur Renauld?"

"Yes."

"Why?"

He shot the question at me with such suddenness that I was taken aback.

"Why?" I stammered. "Why? Oh, because—" I came to a stop.

Poirot nodded his head at me.

"You see, you come to a stumbling block at once. Why should Madame Daubreuil (I shall call her that for clearness' sake) murder Monsieur Renauld? We can find no shadow of a motive. She does not benefit by his death; considered as either mistress or blackmailer she stands to lose.

You cannot have a murder without motive. The first crime was different—there we had a rich lover waiting to step into her husband's shoes."

"Money is not the only motive for murder," I objected.

"True," agreed Poirot placidly. "There are two others, the *crime passionnel* is one. And there is the third rare motive, murder for an idea, which implies some form of mental derangement on the part of the murderer. Homicidal mania and religious fanaticism belong to that class. We can rule it out here."

"But what about the *crime passionnel*? Can you rule that out? If Madame Daubreuil was Renauld's mistress, if she found that his affection was cooling, or if her jealousy was aroused in any way, might she not have struck him down in a moment of anger?"

Poirot shook his head.

"If—I say *if,* you note—Madame Daubreuil was Renauld's mistress, he had not had time to tire of her. And in any case you mistake her character. She is a woman who can simulate great emotional stress. She is a magnificent actress. But, looked at dispassionately, her life disproves her appearance. Throughout, if we examine it, she has been cold-blooded and calculating in her motives and actions. It was not to link her life with that of her young lover that she connived at her husband's murder. The rich American, for whom she probably did not care a button, was her objective. If she committed a crime, she would always do so for gain. Here there was no gain. Besides, how do you account for the digging of the grave? That was a man's work."

"She might have had an accomplice," I suggested, unwilling to relinquish my belief.

"I pass to another objection. You have spoken of the similarity between the two crimes. Wherein does that lie, my friend?"

I stared at him in astonishment.

"Why, Poirot, it was you who remarked on that! The story of the masked men, the 'secret,' the papers!"

Poirot smiled a little.

"Do not be so indignant, I beg of you. I repudiate nothing. The similarity of the two stories links the two cases together inevitably. But reflect now on something very curious. It is not Madame Daubreuil who tells us this tale—if it were, all would indeed be plain sailing—it is Madame Renauld. Is she then in league with the other?"

"I can't believe that," I said slowly. "If she is, she must be the most consummate actress the world has ever known."

"Ta-ta-ta!" said Poirot impatiently. "Again you have the sentiment and not the logic! If it is necessary for a criminal to be a consummate actress, then by all means assume her to be one.

But is it necessary? I do not believe Mrs. Renauld to be in league with Madame Daubreuil for several reasons, some of which I have already enumerated to you. The others are self-evident. Therefore, that possibility eliminated, we draw very near to the truth, which is, as always, very curious and interesting."

"Poirot," I cried, "what more do you know?"

"*Mon ami*, you must make your own deductions. You have 'access to the facts.' Concentrate your grey cells. Reason—not like Giraud—but like Hercule Poirot!"

"But are you *sure?*"

"My friend, in many ways I have been an imbecile. But at last I see clearly."

"You know everything?"

"I have discovered what Monsieur Renauld sent for me to discover."

"And you know the murderer?"

"I know one murderer."

"What do you mean?"

"We talk a little at cross-purposes. There are here not one crime, but two. The first I have solved, the second—*eh bien*, I will confess, I am not sure!"

"But, Poirot, I thought you said the man in the shed had died a natural death?"

"Ta-ta-ta!" Poirot made his favourite ejaculation of impatience. "Still you do not understand. One may have a crime without a murderer, but for

179

two crimes it is essential to have two bodies."

His remark struck me as so peculiarly lacking in lucidity that I looked at him in some anxiety. But he appeared perfectly normal. Suddenly he rose and strolled to the window.

"Here he is," he observed.

"Who?"

"Monsieur Jack Renauld. I sent a note up to the Villa to ask him to come here."

That changed the course of my ideas, and I asked Poirot if he knew that Jack Renauld had been in Merlinville on the night of the crime. I had hoped to catch my astute little friend napping, but as usual he was omniscient. He, too, had inquired at the station.

"And without doubt we are not original in the idea, Hastings. The excellent Giraud, he also has probably made his inquiries."

"You don't think—" I said, and then stopped. "Ah, no, it would be too horrible!"

Poirot looked inquiringly at me, but I said no more. It had just occurred to me that though there were seven women, directly and indirectly connected with the case—Mrs. Renauld, Madame Daubreuil and her daughter, the mysterious visitor, and the three servants—there was, with the exception of old Auguste, who could hardly count, only one man—Jack Renauld. *And a man must have dug the grave.*

I had no time to develop farther the appalling

idea that had occurred to me, for Jack Renauld was ushered into the room.

Poirot greeted him in businesslike manner.

"Take a seat, monsieur. I regret infinitely to derange you, but you will perhaps understand that the atmosphere of the villa is not too congenial to me. Monsieur Giraud and I do not see eye to eye about everything. His politeness to me has not been striking, and you will comprehend that I do not intend any little discoveries I may make to benefit him in any way."

"Exactly, Monsieur Poirot," said the lad. "That fellow Giraud is an ill-conditioned brute, and I'd be delighted to see someone score at his expense."

"Then I may ask a little favour of you?"

"Certainly."

"I will ask you to go to the railway station and take a train to the next station along the line, Abbalac. Ask at the cloakroom whether two foreigners deposited a valise there on the night of the murder. It is a small station, and they are almost certain to remember. Will you do this?"

"Of course I will," said the boy, mystified, though ready for the task.

"I and my friend, you comprehend, have business elsewhere," explained Poirot. "There is a train in a quarter of an hour, and I will ask you not to return to the villa, as I have no wish for Giraud to get an inkling of your errand."

"Very well, I will go straight to the station."

He rose to his feet. Poirot's voice stopped him: "One moment, Monsieur Renauld, there is one little matter that puzzles me. Why did you not mention to Monsieur Hautet this morning that you were in Merlinville on the night of the crime?"

Jack Renauld's face went crimson. With an effort he controlled himself.

"You have made a mistake. I was in Cherbourg as I told the examining magistrate this morning."

Poirot looked at him, his eyes narrowed, catlike, until they only showed a gleam of green.

"Then it is a singular mistake that I have made there—for it is shared by the station staff. They say you arrived by the 11:40 train."

For a moment Jack Renauld hesitated, then he made up his mind.

"And if I did? I suppose you do not mean to accuse me of participating in my father's murder?" He asked the question haughtily, his head thrown back.

"I should like an explanation of the reason that brought you here."

"That is simple enough. I came to see my fiancée, Mademoiselle Daubreuil. I was on the eve of a long voyage, uncertain as to when I should return. I wished to see her before I went, to assure her of my unchanging devotion."

"And did you see her?" Poirot's eyes never left the other's face.

There was an appreciable pause before Renauld replied. Then he said:

"Yes."

"And afterwards?"

"I found I had missed the last train. I walked to St. Beauvais, where I knocked up a garage and got a car to take me back to Cherbourg."

"St. Beauvais? That is fifteen kilometres. A long walk, M. Renauld."

"I—I felt like walking."

Poirot bowed his head as a sign that he accepted the explanation. Jack Renauld took up his hat and cane and departed. In a trice Poirot jumped to his feet.

"Quick, Hastings. We will go after him."

Keeping a discreet distance behind our quarry, we followed him through the streets of Merlinville. But when Poirot saw that he took the turning to the station he checked himself.

"All is well. He has taken the bait. He will go to Abbalac, and will inquire for the mythical valise left by the mythical foreigners. Yes, *mon ami*, all that was a little invention of my own."

"You wanted him out of the way!" I exclaimed.

"Your penetration is amazing, Hastings! Now, if you please, we will go up to the Villa Geneviève."

Eighteen

GIRAUD ACTS

Arrived at the villa, Poirot led the way up to the shed where the second body had been discovered. He did not, however, go in, but paused by the bench which I have mentioned before as being set some few yards away from it. After contemplating it for a moment or two, he paced carefully from it to the hedge which marked the boundary between the Villa Geneviève and the Villa Marguerite. Then he paced back again, nodding his head as he did so. Returning again to the hedge, he parted the bushes with his hands.

"With good fortune," he remarked to me over his shoulder, "Mademoiselle Marthe may find herself in the garden. I desire to speak to her and would prefer not to call formally at the Villa Marguerite. Ah, all is well, there she is. Pst, Mademoiselle! Pst! *Un moment, s'il vous plaît.*"

I joined him at the moment that Marthe Daubreuil, looking slightly startled, came running up to the hedge at his call.

"A little word with you, mademoiselle, if it is permitted?"

"Certainly, Monsieur Poirot."

Despite her acquiescence, her eyes looked troubled and afraid.

"Mademoiselle, do you remember running after me on the road the day that I came to your house with the examining magistrate? You asked me if anyone were suspected of the crime."

"And you told me two Chileans." Her voice sounded rather breathless, and her left hand stole to her breast.

"Will you ask me the same question again, mademoiselle?"

"What do you mean?"

"This. If you were to ask me that question again, I should give you a different answer. Someone is suspected—but not a Chilean."

"Who?" The word came faintly between her parted lips.

"Monsieur Jack Renauld."

"What?" It was a cry. "Jack? Impossible. Who dares to suspect him?"

"Giraud."

"Giraud!" The girl's face was ashy. "I am afraid of that man. He is cruel. He will—he will—" She broke off. There was courage gathering in her face, and determination. I realized in that moment that she was a fighter. Poirot, too, watched her intently.

"You know, of course, that he was here on the night of the murder?" he asked.

"Yes," she replied mechanically. "He told me."

"It was unwise to have tried to conceal the fact," ventured Poirot.

"Yes, yes," she replied impatiently. "But we cannot waste time on regrets. We must find something to save him. He is innocent, of course; but that will not help him with a man like Giraud, who has his reputation to think of. He must arrest someone, and that someone will be Jack."

"The facts will tell against him," said Poirot. "You realize that?"

She faced him squarely.

"I am not a child, monsieur. I can be brave and look facts in the face. He is innocent, and we must save him."

She spoke with a kind of desperate energy, then was silent, frowning as she thought.

"Mademoiselle," said Poirot, observing her keenly, "is there not something that you are keeping back that you could tell us?"

She nodded perplexedly.

"Yes, there is something, but I hardly know whether you will believe it—it seems so absurd."

"At any rate, tell us, mademoiselle."

"It is this. M. Giraud sent for me, as an afterthought, to see if I could identify the man in there." She signed with her head towards the shed. "I could not. At least I could not at the moment. But since I have been thinking—"

"Well?"

"It seems so queer, and yet I am almost sure. I will tell you. On the morning of the day Monsieur Renauld was murdered, I was walking in the garden here, when I heard a sound of men's voices quarrelling. I pushed aside the bushes and looked through. One of the men was Monsieur Renauld and the other was a tramp, a dreadful-looking creature in filthy rags. He was alternately whining and threatening. I gathered he was asking for money, but at that moment *maman* called me from the house, and I had to go. That is all, only—I am almost sure that the tramp and the dead man in the shed are one and the same."

Poirot uttered an exclamation.

"But why did you not say at the time, mademoiselle?"

"Because at first it only struck me that the face was vaguely familiar in some way. The man was differently dressed, and apparently belonged to a superior station in life."

A voice called from the house.

"*Maman,*" whispered Marthe: "I must go." And she slipped away through the trees.

"Come," said Poirot and, taking my arm, turned in the direction of the villa.

"What do you really think?" I asked in some curiosity. "Was that story true, or did the girl make it up in order to divert suspicion from her lover?"

"It is a curious tale," said Poirot, "but I believe it to be the absolute truth. Unwittingly, Mademoiselle Marthe told us the truth on another point—and incidentally gave Jack Renauld the lie. Did you notice his hesitation when I asked him if he saw Marthe Daubreuil on the night of the crime? He paused and then said 'Yes.' I suspected that he was lying. It was necessary for me to see Mademoiselle Marthe before he could put her on her guard. Three little words gave me the information I wanted. When I asked her if she knew that Jack Renauld was here that night, she answered, 'He *told* me.' Now, Hastings, what was Jack Renauld doing here on that eventful evening, and if he did not see Mademoiselle Marthe whom did he see?"

"Surely, Poirot," I cried, aghast, "you cannot believe that a boy like that would murder his own father!"

"*Mon ami*," said Poirot. "You continue to be of a sentimentality unbelievable! I have seen mothers who murdered their little children for the sake of the insurance money! After that, one can believe anything."

"And the motive?"

"Money of course. Remember that Jack Renauld thought that he would come into half his father's fortune at the latter's death."

"But the tramp. Where does he come in?"

Poirot shrugged his shoulders.

"Giraud would say that he was an accomplice— an apache who helped young Renauld to commit the crime, and who was conveniently put out of the way afterwards."

"But the hair round the dagger? The woman's hair?"

"Ah!" said Poirot, smiling broadly. "That is the cream of Giraud's little jest. According to him, it is not a woman's hair at all. Remember that the youths of today wear their hair brushed straight back from the forehead with pomade or hair wash to make it lie flat. Consequently some of the hairs are of considerable length."

"And you believe that too?"

"No," said Poirot, with a curious smile. "For I know it to be the hair of a woman—and more, which woman!"

"Madame Daubreuil," I announced positively.

"Perhaps," said Poirot, regarding me quizzically. But I refused to allow myself to get annoyed.

"What are we going to do now?" I asked, as we entered the hall of the Villa Geneviève.

"I wish to make a search among the effects of M. Jack Renauld. That is why I had to get him out of the way for a few hours."

Neatly and methodically, Poirot opened each drawer in turn, examined the contents, and returned them exactly to their places. It was a singularly dull and uninteresting proceeding. Poirot waded on through collars, pyjamas, and socks. A purring noise outside drew me to the window. Instantly I became galvanized into life.

"Poirot!" I cried. "A car has just driven up.

189

Giraud is in it, and Jack Renauld, and two gendarmes."

"*Sacré tonnerre!*" growled Poirot. "That animal of a Giraud, could he not wait? I shall not be able to replace the things in this last drawer with the proper method. Let us be quick."

Unceremoniously he tumbled out the things on the floor, mostly ties and handkerchiefs. Suddenly with a cry of triumph Poirot pounced on something, a small square of cardboard, evidently a photograph. Thrusting it into his pocket, he returned the things pell-mell to the drawer, and seizing me by the arm dragged me out of the room and down the stairs. In the hall stood Giraud, contemplating his prisoner.

"Good afternoon, Monsieur Giraud," said Poirot. "What have we here?"

Giraud nodded his head towards Jack.

"He was trying to make a getaway, but I was too sharp for him. He's under arrest for the murder of his father, Monsieur Paul Renauld."

Poirot wheeled round to confront the boy, who was leaning limply against the door, his face ashy pale.

"What do you say to that, *jeune homme*?"

Jack Renauld stared at him stonily.

"Nothing," he said.

Nineteen

I Use My Grey Cells

I was dumbfounded. Up to the last, I had not been able to bring myself to believe Jack Renauld guilty. I had expected a ringing proclamation of his innocence when Poirot challenged him. But now, watching him as he stood, white and limp against the wall, and hearing the damning admission fall from his lips, I doubted no longer.

But Poirot had turned to Giraud.

"What are your grounds for arresting him?"

"Do you expect me to give them to you?"

"As a matter of courtesy, yes."

Giraud looked at him doubtfully. He was torn between a desire to refuse rudely and the pleasure of triumphing over his adversary.

"You think I have made a mistake, I suppose?" he sneered.

"It would not surprise me," replied Poirot, with a soupçon of malice.

Giraud's face took on a deeper tinge of red.

"*Eh bien*, come in here. You shall judge for yourself."

He flung open the door of the salon, and we passed in, leaving Jack Renauld in the care of the two other men.

"Now, Monsieur Poirot," said Giraud, laying

his hat on the table, and speaking with the utmost sarcasm, "I will treat you to a little lecture on detective work. I will show how we moderns work."

"*Bien!*" said Poirot, composing himself to listen. "I will show you how admirably the Old Guard can listen." And he leaned back and closed his eyes, opening them for a moment to remark: "Do not fear that I shall sleep. I will attend most carefully."

"Of course," began Giraud, "I soon saw through all that Chilean tomfoolery. Two men were in it— but they were not mysterious foreigners! All that was a blind."

"Very creditable so far, my dear Giraud," murmured Poirot. "Especially after that clever trick of theirs with the match and cigarette end."

Giraud glared, but continued.

"A man must have been connected with the case, in order to dig the grave. There is no man who actually benefits by the crime, but there was a man who *thought* he would benefit. I heard of Jack Renauld's quarrel with his father, and of the threats that he had used. The motive was established. Now as to means. Jack Renauld was in Merlinville that night. He concealed the fact— which turned suspicion into certainty. Then we found a second victim—*stabbed with the same dagger.* We know when that dagger was stolen. Captain Hastings here can fix the time. Jack

Renauld, arriving from Cherbourg, was the only person who could have taken it. I have accounted for all the other members of the household."

Poirot interrupted.

"You are wrong. There is one other person who could have taken the dagger."

"You refer to Monsieur Stonor? He arrived at the front door, in an automobile which had brought him straight from Calais. Ah! believe me, I have looked into everything. Monsieur Jack Renauld arrived by train. An hour elapsed between his arrival and the moment when he presented himself at the house. Without doubt, he saw Captain Hastings and his companion leave the shed, slipped in himself and took the dagger, stabbed his accomplice in the shed—"

"Who was already dead!"

Giraud shrugged his shoulders.

"Possibly he did not observe that. He may have judged him to be sleeping. Without doubt they had a rendezvous. In any case he knew this apparent second murder would greatly complicate the case. It did."

"But it could not deceive Monsieur Giraud," murmured Poirot.

"You mock at me! But I will give you one last irrefutable proof. Madame Renauld's story was false—a fabrication from beginning to end. We believe Madame Renauld to have loved her husband—*yet she lied to shield his murderer.* For whom will a woman lie? Sometimes for herself, usually for the man she loves, *always* for her children. That is the last—the irrefutable proof. You cannot get round it."

Giraud paused, flushed and triumphant. Poirot regarded him steadily.

"That is my case," said Giraud. "What have you to say to it?"

"Only that there is one thing you have failed to take into account."

"What is that?"

"Jack Renauld was presumably acquainted with the planning out of the golf course. He knew that the body would be discovered almost at once, when they started to dig the bunker."

Giraud laughed out loud.

"But it is idiotic what you say there! He wanted the body to be found! Until it was found, he could not presume death, and would have been unable to enter into his inheritance."

I saw a quick flash of green in Poirot's eyes as he rose to his feet.

"Then why bury it?" he asked very softly. "Reflect, Giraud. Since it was to Jack Renauld's advantage that the body should be found without delay, *why dig a grave at all?*"

Giraud did not reply. The question found him unprepared. He shrugged his shoulders as though to intimate that it was of no importance.

Poirot moved towards the door. I followed him.

"There is one more thing that you have failed to take into account," he said over his shoulder.

"What is that?"

"The piece of lead piping," said Poirot, and left the room.

Jack Renauld still stood in the hall, with a white dumb face, but as we came out of the salon he looked up sharply. At the same moment there was the sound of a footfall on the staircase. Mrs. Renauld was descending it. At the sight of her son, standing between the two myrmidons of the law, she stopped as though petrified.

"Jack," she faltered. "Jack, what is this?"

He looked up at her, his face set.

"They have arrested me, mother."

"What?"

She uttered a piercing cry, and before anyone could get to her, swayed, and fell heavily. We both ran to her and lifted her up. In a minute Poirot stood up again.

"She has cut her head badly, on the corner of the stairs. I fancy there is slight concussion also. If Giraud wants a statement from her, he will have to wait. She will probably be unconscious for at least a week."

Denise and Françoise had run to their mistress, and leaving her in their charge Poirot left the house. He walked with his head down, frowning thoughtfully. For some time I did not speak, but at last I ventured to put a question to him:

"Do you believe then, in spite of all appearances to the contrary, that Jack Renauld may not be guilty?"

Poirot did not answer at once, but after a long wait he said gravely:

"I do not know, Hastings. There is just a chance of it. Of course Giraud is all wrong—wrong from beginning to end. If Jack Renauld is guilty, it is in spite of Giraud's arguments, not *because* of them. And the gravest indictment against him is known only to me."

"What is that?" I asked, impressed.

"If you would use your grey cells, and see the whole case clearly as I do, you too would perceive it, my friend."

This was what I called one of Poirot's irritating answers. He went on, without waiting for me to speak:

"Let us walk this way to the sea. We will sit on that little mound there, overlooking the beach, and review the case. You shall know all that I know, but I would prefer that you should come at the truth by your own efforts—not by my leading you by the hand."

We established ourselves on the grassy knoll as Poirot had suggested, looking out to sea.

"Think, my friend," said Poirot's voice encouragingly. "Arrange your ideas. Be methodical. Be orderly. There is the secret of success."

I endeavoured to obey him, casting my mind

back over all the details of the case. And suddenly I started as an idea of bewildering luminosity shot into my brain. Tremblingly I built up my hypothesis.

"You have a little idea, I see, *mon ami*! Capital. We progress."

I sat up, and lit a pipe.

"Poirot," I said, "it seems to me we have been strangely remiss. I say *we*—although I dare say *I* would be nearer the mark. But you must pay the penalty of your determined secrecy. So I say again we have been strangely remiss. There is someone we have forgotten."

"And who is that?" inquired Poirot, with twinkling eyes.

"Georges Conneau!"

Twenty

AN AMAZING STATEMENT

The next moment Poirot embraced me warmly on the cheek.

"*Enfin*! You have arrived! And all by yourself. It is superb! Continue your reasoning. You are right. Decidedly we have done wrong to forget Georges Conneau."

I was so flattered by the little man's approval that I could hardly continue. But at last I collected my thoughts and went on.

"Georges Conneau disappeared twenty years ago, but we have no reason to believe that he is dead."

"*Aucunement,*" agreed Poirot. "Proceed."

"Therefore we will assume that he is alive."

"Exactly."

"Or that he was alive until recently."

"*De mieux en mieux!*"

"We will presume," I continued, my enthusiasm rising, "that he has fallen on evil days. He has become a criminal, an apache, a tramp—a what you will. He chances to come to Merlinville. There he finds the woman he has never ceased to love."

"Eh eh! The sentimentality," warned Poirot.

"Where one hates one also loves," I quoted or misquoted. "At any rate he finds her there, living under an assumed name. But she has a new lover, the Englishman, Renauld. Georges Conneau, the memory of old wrongs rising in him, quarrels with this Renauld. He lies in wait for him as he comes to visit his mistress, and stabs him in the back. Then, terrified at what he has done, he starts to dig a grave. I imagine it likely that Madame Daubreuil comes out to look for her lover. She and Conneau have a terrible scene. He drags her into the shed, and there suddenly falls down in an epileptic fit. Now supposing Jack Renauld to appear. Madame Daubreuil tells him all, points out to him the dreadful consequences to her daughter if this scandal of the past is revived. His father's murderer is dead—let them do their best to hush it up. Jack Renauld consents—goes to the house and has an interview with his mother, winning her over to his point of view. Primed with the story that Madame Daubreuil has suggested to him, she permits herself to be gagged and bound. There, Poirot, what do you think of that?" I leaned back, flushed with the pride of successful reconstruction.

Poirot looked at me thoughtfully.

"I think that you should write for the Kinema, *mon ami*," he remarked at last.

"You mean—"

"It would mean a good film, the story that you have recounted to me there—but it bears no sort of resemblance to everyday life."

"I admit that I haven't gone into all the details, but—"

"You have gone farther—you have ignored them magnificently. What about the way the two men were dressed? Do you suggest that after stabbing his victim, Conneau removed his suit of clothes, donned it himself, and replaced the dagger?"

"I don't see that that matters," I objected rather huffily. "He may have obtained clothes and money from Madame Daubreuil by threats earlier in the day."

"By threats—eh? You seriously advance that supposition?"

"Certainly. He could have threatened to reveal her identity to the Renaulds, which would probably have put an end to all hopes of her daughter's marriage."

"You are wrong, Hastings. He could not blackmail her, for she had the whip hand. Georges Conneau, remember, is still wanted for murder. A word from her and he is in danger of the guillotine."

I was forced, rather reluctantly, to admit the truth of this.

"*Your* theory," I remarked acidly, "is doubtless correct as to all the details?"

"My theory is the truth," said Poirot quietly. "And the truth is necessarily correct. In your theory you made a fundamental error. You permitted your imagination to lead you astray with midnight assignations and passionate love scenes. But in investigating crime we must take our stand upon the commonplace. Shall I demonstrate my methods to you?"

"Oh, by all means let us have a demonstration!"

Poirot sat very upright and began, wagging his forefinger emphatically to emphasize his points:

"I will start as you started from the basic fact of Georges Conneau. Now the story told by Madame Beroldy in court as to the 'Russians' was admittedly a fabrication. If she was innocent of connivance in the crime, it was concocted by her, and by her only as she stated. If, on the other hand, she was *not* innocent, it might have been invented by either her or Georges Conneau.

"Now, in this case we are investigating, we meet the same tale. As I pointed out to you, the facts render it very unlikely that Madame Daubreuil inspired it. So we turn to the hypothesis that the story had its origin in the brain of Georges Conneau. Very good. Georges Conneau, therefore, planned the crime, with Mrs. Renauld as his accomplice. She is in the limelight, and behind her is a shadowy figure whose present *alias* is unknown to us.

"Now let us go carefully over the Renauld Case from the beginning, setting down each significant point in its chronological order. You have a notebook and pencil? Good. Now what is the earliest point to note down?"

"The letter to you?"

"That was the first we knew of it, but it is not the proper beginning of the case. The first point of any significance, I should say, is the change that came over Monsieur Renauld shortly after arriving in Merlinville, and which is attested to by several witnesses. We have also to consider his friendship with Madame Daubreuil, and the large sums of money paid over to her. From thence we can come directly to the 23rd May."

Poirot paused, cleared his throat, and signed to me to write:

"*23rd May.* M. Renauld quarrels with his son

over latter's wish to marry Marthe Daubreuil. Son leaves for Paris.

"*24th May.* M. Renauld alters his will, leaving entire control of his fortune in his wife's hands.

"*7th June.* Quarrel with tramp in garden, witnessed by Marthe Daubreuil.

"Letter written to M. Hercule Poirot, imploring assistance.

"Telegram sent to M. Jack Renauld, bidding him proceed by the *Anzora* to Buenos Aires.

"Chauffeur, Masters, sent off on a holiday.

"Visit of a lady that evening. As he is seeing her out, his words are 'Yes, yes—but for God's sake go now. . . .' "

Poirot paused.

"There, Hastings, take each of those facts one by one, consider them carefully by themselves and in relation to the whole, and see if you do not get new light on the matter."

I endeavoured conscientiously to do as he had said. After a moment or two, I said rather doubtfully:

"As to the first points, the question seems to be whether we adopt the theory of blackmail, or of an infatuation for this woman."

"Blackmail, decidedly. You heard what Stonor said as to his character and habits."

"Mrs. Renauld did not confirm his view," I argued.

"We have already seen that Madame Renauld's

testimony cannot be relied upon in any way. We must trust to Stonor on that point."

"Still, if Renauld had an affair with a woman called Bella, there seems no inherent improbability in his having another with Madame Daubreuil."

"None whatever, I grant you, Hastings. But did he?"

"The letter, Poirot. You forget the letter."

"No, I do not forget. But what makes you think that letter was written to Monsieur Renauld?"

"Why, it was found in his pocket, and—and—"

"And that is all!" cut in Poirot. "There was no mention of any name to show to whom the letter was addressed. We assumed it was to the dead man because it was in the pocket of his overcoat. Now, *mon ami*, something about that overcoat struck me as unusual. I measured it, and made the remark that he wore his overcoat very long. That remark should have given you to think."

"I thought you were just saying it for the sake of saying something," I confessed.

"Ah, *quelle idée*! Later you observed me measuring the overcoat of Monsieur Jack Renauld. *Eh bien*, Monsieur Jack Renauld wears his overcoat very short. Put those two facts together with a third, namely, that Monsieur Jack Renauld flung out of the house in a hurry on his departure for Paris, and tell me what you make of it!"

"I see," I said slowly, as the meaning of Poirot's remarks bore in upon me. "That letter was written to Jack Renauld—not to his father. He caught up the wrong overcoat in his haste and agitation."

Poirot nodded.

"*Précisément*! We can return to this point later. For the moment let us content ourselves with accepting the letter as having nothing to do with Monsieur Renauld *père*, and pass to the next chronological event."

" '*23rd May.*' " I read: " 'M. Renauld quarrels with his son over latter's wish to marry Marthe Daubreuil. Son leaves for Paris.' I don't see anything much to remark upon there, and the altering of the will the following day seems straightforward enough. It was the direct result of the quarrel."

"We agree, *mon ami*—at least as to the cause. But what exact motive underlay this procedure of Monsieur Renauld's?"

I opened my eyes in surprise.

"Anger against his son of course."

"Yet he wrote him affectionate letters to Paris?"

"So Jack Renauld says, but he cannot produce them."

"Well, let us pass from that."

"Now we come to the day of the tragedy. You have placed the events of the morning in a certain order. Have you any justification for that?"

"I have ascertained that the letter to me was

204

posted at the same time as the telegram was dispatched. Masters was informed he could take a holiday shortly afterwards. In my opinion the quarrel with the tramp took place anterior to these happenings."

"I do not see that you can fix that definitely unless you question Madame Daubreuil again."

"There is no need. I am sure of it. And if you do not see that, you see nothing, Hastings!"

I looked at him for a moment.

"Of course! I am an idiot. If the tramp was Georges Conneau, it was after the stormy interview with him that Mr. Renauld apprehended danger. He sent away the chauffeur, Masters, whom he suspected of being in the other's pay, he wired to his son, and sent for you."

A faint smile crossed Poirot's lips.

"You do not think it strange that he should use exactly the same expressions in his letter as Madame Renauld used, later in her story? If the mention of Santiago was a blind, why should Renauld speak of it, and—what is more—send his son there?"

"It is puzzling, I admit, but perhaps we shall find some explanation later. We come now to the evening, and the visit of the mysterious lady. I confess that that fairly baffles me, unless it was indeed Madame Daubreuil, as Françoise all along maintained."

Poirot shook his head.

"My friend, my friend, where are your wits wandering? Remember the fragment of cheque, and the fact that the name Bella Duveen was faintly familiar to Stonor, and I think we may take it for granted that Bella Duveen is the full name of Jack's unknown correspondent, and that it was she who came to the Villa Geneviève that night. Whether she intended to see Jack, or whether she meant all along to appeal to his father, we cannot be certain, but I think we may assume that this is what occurred. She produced her claim upon Jack, probably showed letters that he had written her, and the older man tried to buy her off by writing a cheque. This she indignantly tore up. The terms of her letter are those of a woman genuinely in love, and she would probably deeply resent being offered money. In the end he got rid of her, and here the words that he used are significant."

" 'Yes, yes, but for God's sake go now,' " I repeated. "They seem to me a little vehement, perhaps, that is all."

"That is enough. He was desperately anxious for the girl to go. Why? Not because the interview was unpleasant. No, it was the time that was slipping by, and for some reason time was precious."

"Why should it be?" I asked bewildered.

"That is what we ask ourselves. Why should it be? But later we have the incident of the wristwatch—which again shows us that time plays a very important part in the crime. We are now fast approaching the actual drama. It is half past ten when Bella Duveen leaves, and by the evidence of the wristwatch we know that the crime was committed, or at any rate that it was staged, before twelve o'clock. We have reviewed all the events anterior to the murder, there remains only one unplaced. By the doctor's evidence, the tramp, when found, had been dead at least forty-eight hours—with a possible margin of twenty-four hours more. Now, with no other facts to help me than those we have discussed, I place the death as having occurred on the morning of 7th June."

I stared at him, stupefied.

"But how? Why? How can you possibly know?"

"Because only in that way can the sequence of events be logically explained. *Mon ami*, I have taken you step by step along the way. Do you not now see what is so glaringly plain?"

"My dear Poirot, I can't see anything glaring about it. I did think I was beginning to see my way before, but I'm now hopelessly fogged. For goodness' sake, get on, and tell me who killed Mr. Renauld."

"That is just what I am not sure of as yet."

"But you said it was glaringly clear!"

"We talk at cross-purposes, my friend.

Remember, it is *two* crimes we are investigating—for which, as I pointed out to you, we have the necessary two bodies. There, there, *ne vous impatientez pas*! I explain all. To begin with, we apply our psychology. We find three points at which Monsieur Renauld displays a distinct change of view and action—three psychological points therefore. The first occurs immediately after arriving in Merlinville, the second after quarrelling with his son on a certain subject, the third on the morning of 7th June. Now for the three causes. We can attribute No 1 to meeting Madame Daubreuil. No 2 is indirectly connected with her, since it concerns a marriage between Monsieur Renauld's son and her daughter. But the cause of No 3 is hidden from us. We had to deduce it. Now, *mon ami*, let me ask you a question: whom do we believe to have planned this crime?"

"Georges Conneau," I said doubtfully, eyeing Poirot warily.

"Exactly. Now Giraud laid it down as an axiom that a woman lies to save herself, the man she loves, and her child. Since we are satisfied that it was Georges Conneau who dictated the lie to her, and as Georges Conneau is not Jack Renauld, it follows that the third case is put out of court. And, still attributing the crime to Georges Conneau, the first is equally so. So we are forced to the second—that Madame Renauld lied for the sake of the man she loved—or in other words, for the sake of Georges Conneau. You agree to that?"

"Yes," I admitted. "It seems logical enough."

"*Bien*! Madame Renauld loves Georges Conneau. Who, then, is Georges Conneau?"

"The tramp."

"Have we any evidence to show that Madame Renauld loved the tramp?"

"No, but—"

"Very well then. Do not cling to theories where facts no longer support them. Ask yourself instead whom Madame Renauld *did* love."

I shook my head perplexed.

"*Mais oui*, you know perfectly. Whom did Madame Renauld love so dearly that when she saw his dead body she fell down in a swoon?"

I stared dumbfounded.

"Her husband?" I gasped.

Poirot nodded.

"Her husband—or Georges Conneau, which-ever you like to call him."

I rallied myself.

"But it's impossible."

"How 'impossible'? Did we not agree just now that Madame Daubreuil was in a position to blackmail Georges Conneau?"

"Yes, but—"

"And did she not very effectively blackmail Monsieur Renauld?"

"That may be true enough, but—"

"And is it not a fact that we know nothing of Monsieur Renauld's youth and upbringing? That he springs suddenly into existence as a French-Canadian exactly twenty-two years ago?"

"All that is so," I said more firmly, "but you seem to me to be overlooking one salient point."

"What is that, my friend?"

"Why, we have admitted that Georges planned the crime. That brings us to the ridiculous statement *that he planned his own murder!*"

"*Eh bien, mon ami,*" said Poirot placidly, "that is just what he did do!"

Twenty-one

HERCULE POIROT ON THE CASE

In a measured voice Poirot began his exposition.

"It seems strange to you, *mon ami*, that a man should plan his own death? So strange, that you prefer to reject the truth as fantastic, and to revert to a story that is in reality ten times more impossible. Yes, Monsieur Renauld planned his own death, but there is one detail that perhaps escapes you—he did not intend to die."

I shook my head, bewildered.

"But no, it is all most simple really," said Poirot kindly. "For the crime that Monsieur Renauld proposed a murderer was not necessary, as I told you, but a body was. Let us reconstruct, seeing events this time from a different angle.

"Georges Conneau flies from justice—to Canada. There, under an assumed name, he marries, and finally acquires a vast fortune in South America. But there is a nostalgia upon him for his own country. Twenty years have elapsed, he is considerably changed in appearance, besides being a man of such eminence that no one is likely to connect him with a fugitive from justice many years ago. He deems it quite safe to return. He takes up his headquarters in England, but intends to spend the summers in France. And ill fortune, or that obscure justice which shapes men's ends and will not allow them to evade the consequences of their acts, takes him to Merlinville. There, in the whole of France, is the one person who is capable of recognizing him. It is, of course, a gold mine to Madame Daubreuil, and a gold mine of which she is not slow to take advantage. He is helpless, absolutely in her power. And she bleeds him heavily.

"And then the inevitable happens. Jack Renauld falls in love with the beautiful girl he sees almost daily, and wishes to marry her. That rouses his father. At all costs, he will prevent his son marrying the daughter of this evil woman. Jack Renauld knows nothing of his father's past, but Madame Renauld knows everything. She is a woman of great force of character and passionately devoted to her husband. They take counsel together. Renauld sees only one way of escape—death. He must appear to die, in reality escaping to another country where he will start again under an assumed name and where Madame Renauld, having played the widow's part for a while, can join him. It is essential that she should have control of the money, so he alters his will. How they meant to manage the body business originally, I do not know—possibly an art student's skeleton and a fire—or something of the kind, but long before their plans have matured an event occurs which plays into their hands. A rough tramp, violent and abusive, finds his way into the garden. There is a struggle, Renauld seeks to eject him, and suddenly the tramp, an epileptic, falls down in a fit. He is dead. Renauld calls his wife. Together they drag him into the shed—as we know the event had occurred just outside—and they realize the marvellous opportunity that has been vouchsafed them. The man bears no resemblance to Renauld but he is middle-aged, of a usual French type. That is sufficient.

"I rather fancy that they sat on the bench up there, out of earshot from the house, discussing matters. Their plan was quickly made. The identification must rest solely on Madame Renauld's evidence. Jack Renauld and the chauffeur (who had been with his master two years) must be got out of the way. It was unlikely that the French women servants would go near the body, and in any case Renauld intended to take measures to deceive anyone not likely to appreciate details. Masters was sent off, a telegram dispatched to Jack, Buenos Aires being selected to give credence to the story that Renauld had decided upon. Having heard of me as a rather obscure elderly detective, he wrote his appeal for help, knowing that when I arrived, the production of the letter would have a profound effect upon the examining magistrate—which, of course, it did.

"They dressed the body of the tramp in a suit of Renauld's and left his ragged coat and trousers by the door of the shed, not daring to take them into the house. And then, to give credence to the tale Madame Renauld was to tell, they drove the aeroplane dagger through his heart. That night Renauld will first bind and gag his wife, and then, taking a spade, will dig a grave in that particular plot of ground where he knows a—how do you call it?—bunkair? is to be made. It is essential that the body should be found—Madame Daubreuil must have no suspicions. On the other hand, if a little time elapses, any dangers as to identity will be greatly lessened. Then, Renauld will don the tramp's rags, and shuffle off to the station, where he will leave, unnoticed, by the 12:10 train. Since the crime will be supposed to have taken place two hours later, no suspicion can possibly attach to him.

"You see now his annoyance at the inopportune visit of the girl, Bella. Every moment of delay is fatal to his plans. He gets rid of her as soon as he can, however. Then, to work! He leaves the front door slightly ajar to create the impression that assassins left that way. He binds and gags Madame Renauld, correcting his mistake of twenty-two years ago, when the looseness of the bonds caused suspicion to fall upon his accomplice, but leaving her primed with essentially the same story as he had invented before, proving the unconscious recoil of the mind against originality. The night is chilly, and he slips on an overcoat over his underclothing, intending to cast it into the grave with the dead man. He goes out by the window, smoothing over the flower bed carefully, and thereby furnishing the most positive evidence against himself. He goes out on to the lonely golf links, and he digs— And then—"

"Yes?"

"And then," said Poirot gravely, "the justice that he has so long eluded overtakes him. An unknown hand stabs him in the back . . . Now, Hastings, you understand what I mean when I talk of *two* crimes. The first crime, the crime that Monsieur Renauld, in his arrogance, asked us to investigate, is solved. But behind it lies a deeper riddle. And to solve that will be difficult—since the criminal, in his wisdom, has been content to avail himself of the devices prepared by Renauld. It has been a particularly perplexing and baffling mystery to solve."

"You're marvellous, Poirot," I said, with admiration. "Absolutely marvellous. No one on earth but you would have done it!"

I think my praise pleased him. For once in his life he looked almost embarrassed.

"That poor Giraud," said Poirot, trying unsuccessfully to look modest. "Without doubt it is not all stupidity. He has had *la mauvaise chance* once or twice. That dark hair coiled round the dagger, for instance. To say the least, it was misleading."

"To tell you the truth, Poirot," I said slowly, "even now I don't quite see—whose hair was it?"

"Madame Renauld's, of course. That is where *la mauvaise chance* came in. Her hair, dark originally, is almost completely silvered. It might just as easily have been a grey hair—and then, by no conceivable effort could Giraud have persuaded himself it came from the head of Jack Renauld! But it is all of a piece. Always the facts must be twisted to fit the theory!

"Without doubt, when Madame Renauld recovers, she will speak. The possibility of her son being accused of the murder never occurred to her. How should it, when she believed him safely at sea on board the *Anzora*? *Ah! voilà une femme*, Hastings! What force, what self-command! She only made one slip. On his unexpected return: 'It does not matter—*now.*' And no one noticed—no one realized the significance of those words. What a terrible part she has had to play, poor woman. Imagine the shock when she goes to identify the body and, instead of what she expects, sees the actual lifeless form of the husband she has believed miles away by now. No wonder she fainted! But since then, despite her grief and her despair, how resolutely she has played her part and how the anguish of it must wring her. She cannot say a word to set us on the track of the real murderers. For her son's sake, no one must know that Paul Renauld was Georges Conneau, the criminal. Final and most bitter blow, she has admitted publicly that Madame Daubreuil was her husband's mistress—for a hint of blackmail might be fatal to her secret. How cleverly she dealt with the examining magistrate when he asked her if there was any mystery in her husband's past life. 'Nothing so romantic, I am sure, monsieur.' It was perfect, the indulgent tone, the soupçon of sad mockery. At once Monsieur Hautet felt himself foolish and melodramatic. Yes, she is a great woman! If she loved a criminal, she loved him royally!"

Poirot lost himself in contemplation.

"One thing more, Poirot, what about the piece of lead-piping?"

"You do not see? To disfigure the victim's face so that it would be unrecognizable. It was that which first set me on the right track. And that imbecile of a Giraud, swarming all over it to look for match ends! Did I not tell you that a clue of two foot long was quite as good as a clue of two inches? You see, Hastings, we must now start again. Who killed Monsieur Renauld? Someone who was near the villa just before twelve o'clock that night, someone who would benefit by his death—the description fits Jack Renauld only too well. The crime need not have been premeditated. And then the dagger!"

I started, I had not realized that point.

"Of course," I said, "Mrs. Renauld's dagger was the second one we found in the tramp. There *were* two, then?"

"Certainly, and since they were duplicates, it stands to reason that Jack Renauld was the owner. But that would not trouble me so much. In fact, I had a little idea as to that. No, the worst indictment against him is again psychological—heredity, *mon ami*, heredity! Like father, like son—Jack Renauld, when all is said or done, is the son of Georges Conneau."

His tone was grave and earnest, and I was impressed in spite of myself.

"What is your little idea that you mentioned just now?" I asked.

For answer, Poirot consulted his turnip-faced watch, and then asked:

"What time is the afternoon boat from Calais?"

"About five, I believe."

"That will do very well. We shall just have time."

"You are going to England?"

"Yes, my friend."

"Why?"

"To find a possible—witness."

"Who?"

With a rather peculiar smile upon his face, Poirot replied:

"Miss Bella Duveen."

"But how will you find her—what do you know about her?"

"I know nothing about her—but I can guess a good deal. We may take it for granted that her name *is* Bella Duveen, and since that name was faintly familiar to Monsieur Stonor, though evidently not in connexion with the Renauld family, it is probable that she is on the stage. Jack Renauld was a young man with plenty of money, and twenty years of age. The stage is sure to have been the home of his first love. It tallies, too, with Monsieur Renauld's attempt to placate her with a cheque. I think I shall find her all right—especially with the help of *this*."

And he brought out the photograph I had seen him take from Jack Renauld's drawer. "With love from Bella" was scrawled across the corner, but it was not that which held my eyes fascinated. The likeness was not first rate—but for all that it was unmistakable to me. I felt a cold sinking, as though some unutterable calamity had befallen me.

It was the face of Cinderella.

Twenty-two

I FIND LOVE

For a moment or two I sat as though frozen, the photograph still in my hand. Then summoning all my courage to appear unmoved, I handed it back. At the same time I stole a quick glance at Poirot. Had he noticed anything? But to my relief he did not seem to be observing me. Anything unusual in my manner had certainly escaped him.

He rose briskly to his feet.

"We have no time to lose. We must make our departure with all dispatch. All is well—the sea it will be calm!"

In the bustle of departure, I had no time for thinking, but once on board the boat, secure from Poirot's observation, I pulled myself together, and attacked the facts dispassionately. How much did Poirot know, and why was he bent on finding this girl? Did he suspect her of having seen Jack Renauld commit the crime? Or did he suspect— But that was impossible! The girl had no grudge against the elder Renauld, no possible motive for wishing his death. What had brought her back to the scene of the murder? I went over the facts carefully. She must have left the train at Calais where I parted from her that day. No wonder I had been unable to find her on the boat. If she had dined in Calais, and then taken a train out to Merlinville, she would have arrived at the Villa Geneviève just about the time that Françoise said. What had she done when she left the house just after ten? Presumably either gone to an hotel, or returned to Calais. And then? The crime had been committed on Tuesday night. On Thursday morning she was once more in Merlinville. Had she ever left France at all? I doubted it very much. What kept her there—the hope of seeing Jack Renauld? I had told her (as at the time we believed) that he was on the high seas *en route* to Buenos Aires. Possibly she was aware that the *Anzora* had not sailed. But to know that she must have seen Jack. Was that what Poirot was after? Had Jack Renauld, returning to see Marthe Daubreuil, come face to face instead with Bella Duveen, the girl he had heartlessly thrown over?

I began to see daylight. If that were indeed the case, it might furnish Jack with the alibi he needed. Yet under those circumstances his silence seemed difficult to explain. Why could he not have spoken out boldly? Did he fear for this former entanglement of his to come to the ears of Marthe Daubreuil? I shook my head, dissatisfied. The thing had been harmless enough, a foolish boy-and-girl affair, and I reflected cynically that the son of a millionaire was not likely to be thrown over by a penniless French girl, who moreover loved him devotedly, without a much graver cause.

Poirot reappeared brisk and smiling at Dover, and our journey to London was uneventful. It was past nine o'clock when we arrived, and I supposed that we should return straight away to our rooms and do nothing till the morning.

But Poirot had other plans.

"We must lose no time, *mon ami*. The news of the arrest will not be in the English papers until the day after tomorrow, but still we must lose no time."

I did not quite follow his reasoning, but I merely asked how he proposed to find the girl.

"You remember Joseph Aarons, the theatrical agent? No? I assisted him in a little matter of a Japanese wrestler. A pretty little problem, I must recount it to you one day. He, without doubt, will be able to put us in the way of finding out what we want to know."

It took us some time to run Mr. Aarons to earth, and it was after midnight when we finally managed it. He greeted Poirot with every evidence of warmth, and professed himself ready to be of service to us in any way.

"There's not much about the profession I don't know," he said, beaming genially.

"*Eh bien*, Monsieur Aarons, I desire to find a young girl called Bella Duveen."

"Bella Duveen. I know the name, but for a moment I can't place it. What's her line?"

"That I do not know—but here is her photograph."

Mr. Aarons studied it for a moment, then his face lighted.

"Got it!" He slapped his thigh. "The Dulcibella Kids, by the Lord!"

"The Dulcibella Kids?"

"That's it. They're sisters. Acrobats, dancers, and singers. Give quite a good little turn. They're in the provinces, somewhere, I believe—if they're not resting. They've been on in Paris for the last two or three weeks."

"Can you find out for me exactly where they are?"

"Easy as a bird. You go home, and I'll send you round the dope in the morning."

With this promise we took leave of him. He was as good as his word. About eleven o'clock the following day, a scribbled note reached us.

"The Dulcibella Sisters are on at the Palace in Coventry. Good luck to you."

Without more ado, we started for Coventry. Poirot made no inquiries at the theatre, but contented himself with booking stalls for the variety performance that evening.

The show was wearisome beyond words—or perhaps it was only my mood that made it seem so. Japanese families balanced themselves precariously, would-be fashionable men, in greenish evening dress and exquisitely slicked hair, reeled off society patter and danced marvellously. Stout prima donnas sang at the top of the human register, a comic comedian endeavoured to be Mr. George Robey and failed signally.

At last the number went up which announced the Dulcibella Kids. My heart beat sickeningly. There she was—there they both were, the pair of them, one flaxen-haired, one dark, matching as to size, with short fluffy skirts and immense "Buster Brown" bows. They looked a pair of extremely piquant children. They began to sing. Their voices were fresh and true, rather thin and music-hally, but attractive.

It was quite a pretty little turn. They danced neatly, and did some clever little acrobatic feats. The words of their songs were crisp and catchy. When the curtain fell, there was a full meed of applause. Evidently the Dulcibella Kids were a success.

Suddenly I felt that I could remain no longer. I

must get out into the air. I suggested leaving to Poirot.

"Go by all means, *mon ami*. I amuse myself, and will stay to the end. I will rejoin you later."

It was only a few steps from the theatre to the hotel. I went up to the sitting room, ordered a whisky and soda, and sat drinking it, staring meditatively into the empty grate. I heard the door open, and turned my head, thinking it was Poirot. Then I jumped to my feet. It was Cinderella who stood in the doorway. She spoke haltingly, her breath coming in little gasps.

"I saw you in front. You and your friend. When you got up to go, I was waiting outside and followed you. Why are you here—in Coventry? What were you doing there tonight? Is the man who was with you the—the detective?"

She stood there, the cloak she had wrapped round her stage dress slipping from her shoulders. I saw the whiteness of her cheeks under the rouge, and heard the terror in her voice. And in that moment I understood everything—understood why Poirot was seeking her, and what she feared, and understood at last my own heart. . . .

"Yes," I said gently.

"Is he looking for—me?" she half whispered.

Then, as I did not answer for a moment, she slipped down by the big chair, and burst into violent bitter weeping.

I knelt down by her, holding her in my arms, and smoothing the hair back from her face.

"Don't cry, child, don't cry, for God's sake. You're safe here. I'll take care of you. Don't cry, darling. Don't cry. I know—I know everything."

"Oh, but you don't!"

"I think I do." And after a moment, as her sobs grew quieter, I asked: "It was you who took the dagger, wasn't it?"

"Yes."

"That was why you wanted me to show you round? And why you pretended to faint?"

Again she nodded.

"Why did you take the dagger?" I asked presently.

She replied as simply as a child:

"I was afraid there might be fingermarks on it."

"But didn't you remember that you had worn gloves?"

She shook her head as though bewildered, and then said slowly:

"Are you going to give me up to—to the police?"

"Good God! no."

Her eyes sought mine long and earnestly, and then she asked in a little quiet voice that sounded afraid of itself:

"Why not?"

It seemed a strange place and a strange time for a declaration of love—and God knows, in all my imagining, I had never pictured love coming to me in such a guise. But I answered simply and naturally enough:

"Because I love you, Cinderella."

She bent her head down, as though ashamed, and muttered in a broken voice:

"You can't—you can't—not if you knew—" And then, as though rallying herself, she faced me squarely, and asked, "What do you know, then?"

"I know that you came to see Mr. Renauld that night. He offered you a cheque and you tore it up indignantly. Then you left the house—" I paused.

"Go on—what next?"

"I don't know whether you knew Jack Renauld would be coming that night, or whether you just waited about on the chance of seeing him, but you did wait about. Perhaps you were just miserable and walked aimlessly—but at any rate just before twelve you were still near there, and you saw a man on the golf links—"

Again I paused. I had leapt to the truth in a flash as she entered the room, but now the picture rose before me even more convincingly. I saw vividly the peculiar pattern of the overcoat on the dead body of Mr. Renauld, and I remembered the amazing likeness that had startled me into believing for one instant that the dead man had risen from the dead when his son burst into our conclave in the salon.

"Go on," repeated the girl steadily.

"I fancy his back was to you—but you recognized him, or thought you recognized him. The gait and the carriage were familiar to you, and the pattern of his overcoat." I paused. "You used a threat in one of your letters to Jack Renauld. When you saw him there, your anger and jealousy drove you mad—and you struck! I don't believe for a minute that you meant to kill him. But you did kill him, Cinderella."

She had flung up her hands to cover her face, and in a choked voice she said:

"You're right . . . you're right . . . I can see it all as you tell it." Then she turned on me almost savagely. "And you love me? Knowing what you do, how can you love me?"

"I don't know," I said a little wearily. "I think love is like that—a thing one cannot help. I have tried, I know—ever since the first day I met you. And love has been too strong for me."

And then suddenly, when I least expected it, she broke down again, casting herself down on the floor and sobbing wildly.

"Oh, I can't!" she cried. "I don't know what to do. I don't know which way to turn. Oh, pity me, pity me, someone, and tell me what to do!"

Again I knelt by her, soothing her as best I could.

"Don't be afraid of me, Bella. For God's sake don't be afraid of me. I love you, that's true—but

I don't want anything in return. Only let me help you. Love him still if you have to, but let me help you, as he can't."

It was as though she had been turned to stone by my words. She raised her head from her hands and stared at me.

"You think that?" she whispered. "You think that I love Jack Renauld?"

Then, half laughing, half crying, she flung her arms passionately round my neck, and pressed her sweet wet face to mine.

"Not as I love you," she whispered. "Never as I love you!"

Her lips brushed my cheek, and then, seeking my mouth, kissed me again and again with a sweetness and fire beyond belief. The wildness of it—and the wonder, I shall not forget—no, not as long as I live!

It was a sound in the doorway that made us look up. Poirot was standing there looking at us.

I did not hesitate. With a bound I reached him and pinioned his arms to his sides.

"Quick," I said to the girl. "Get out of here. As fast as you can. I'll hold him."

With one look at me, she fled out of the room past us. I held Poirot in a grip of iron.

"*Mon ami,*" observed the latter mildly, "you do this sort of thing very well. The strong man holds me in his grasp and I am helpless as a child. But all this is uncomfortable and slightly ridiculous. Let us sit down and be calm."

"You won't pursue her?"

"*Mon Dieu*! no. Am I Giraud? Release me, my friend."

Keeping a suspicious eye upon him, for I paid Poirot the compliment of knowing that I was no match for him in astuteness, I relaxed my grip, and he sank into an armchair, feeling his arms tenderly.

"It is that you have the strength of a bull when you are roused, Hastings! *Eh bien*, and do you think you have behaved well to your old friend? I show you the girl's photograph and you recognize it, but you never say a word."

"There was no need if you knew that I recognized it," I said rather bitterly. So Poirot had known all along! I had not deceived him for an instant.

"Ta-ta! You did not know that I knew that. And tonight you help the girl to escape when we have found her with so much trouble. *Eh bien*! it comes to this—are you going to work with me or against me, Hastings?"

For a moment or two I did not answer. To break with my old friend gave me great pain. Yet I must definitely range myself against him. Would he ever forgive me, I wondered? He had been strangely calm so far, but I knew him to possess marvellous self-command.

"Poirot," I said, "I'm sorry. I admit I've behaved badly to you over this. But sometimes one has no choice. And in future I must take my own line."

Poirot nodded his head several times.

"I understand," he said. The mocking light had quite died out of his eyes, and he spoke with a sincerity and kindness that surprised me. "It is that, my friend, is it not? It is love that has come—not as you imagined it, all cock-a-hoop with fine feathers, but sadly, with bleeding feet. Well, well—I warned you. When I realized that this girl must have taken the dagger, I warned you. Perhaps you remember. But already it was too late. But, tell me, how much do you know?"

I met his eyes squarely.

"Nothing that you could tell me would be any surprise to me, Poirot. Understand that. But in case you think of resuming your search for Miss Duveen, I should like you to know one thing clearly. If you have any idea that she was concerned in the crime, or was the mysterious lady who called upon Mr. Renauld that night, you are wrong. I travelled home from France with her that day, and parted from her at Victoria that evening, so that it is clearly impossible for her to have been in Merlinville."

"Ah!" Poirot looked at me thoughtfully. "And you would swear to that in a court of law?"

"Most certainly I would."

Poirot rose and bowed.

"*Mon ami*! *Vive l'amour*! It can perform miracles. It is decidedly ingenious what you have thought of there. It defeats even Hercule Poirot!"

Twenty-three

DIFFICULTIES AHEAD

After a moment of stress, such as I have just described, reaction is bound to set in. I retired to rest that night on a note of triumph, but I awoke to realize that I was by no means out of the wood. True, I could see no flaw in the alibi I had so suddenly conceived. I had but to stick to my story, and I failed to see how Bella could be convicted in face of it.

But I felt the need of treading warily. Poirot would not take defeat lying down. Somehow or other, he would endeavour to turn the tables on me, and that in the way, and at the moment, when I least expected it.

We met at breakfast the following morning as though nothing had happened. Poirot's good temper was imperturbable, yet I thought I detected a film of reserve in his manner which was new. After breakfast, I announced my intention of going out for a stroll. A malicious gleam shot through Poirot's eyes.

"If it is information you seek, you need not be

at the pains of deranging yourself. I can tell you all you wish to know. The Dulcibella Sisters have cancelled their contract, and have left Coventry for an unknown destination."

"Is that really so, Poirot?"

"You can take it from me, Hastings. I made inquiries the first thing this morning. After all, what else did you expect?"

True enough, nothing else could be expected under the circumstances. Cinderella had profited by the slight start I had been able to secure her, and would certainly not lose a moment in removing herself from the reach of the pursuer. It was what I had intended and planned. Nevertheless, I was aware of being plunged into a network of fresh difficulties.

I had absolutely no means of communicating with the girl, and it was vital that she should know the line of defence that had occurred to me, and which I was prepared to carry out. Of course it was possible that she might try to send word to me in some way or another, but I hardly thought it likely. She would know the risk she ran of a message being intercepted by Poirot, thus setting him on her track once more. Clearly her only course was to disappear utterly for the time being.

But, in the meantime, what was Poirot doing? I studied him attentively. He was wearing his most innocent air, and staring meditatively into the far distance. He looked altogether too placid and supine to give me reassurance. I had learned, with Poirot, that the less dangerous he looked, the more dangerous he was. His quiescence alarmed me. Observing a troubled quality in my glance, he smiled benignantly.

"You are puzzled, Hastings? You ask yourself why I do not launch myself in pursuit?"

"Well—something of the kind."

"It is what you would do, were you in my place. I understand that. But I am not of those who enjoy rushing up and down a country seeking a needle in a haystack, as you English say. No—let Mademoiselle Bella Duveen go. Without doubt, I shall be able to find her when the time comes. Until then, I am content to wait."

I stared at him doubtfully. Was he seeking to mislead me? I had an irritating feeling that, even now, he was master of the situation. My sense of superiority was gradually waning. I had contrived the girl's escape, and evolved a brilliant scheme for saving her from the consequences of her rash act—but I could not rest easy in my mind. Poirot's perfect calm awakened a thousand apprehensions.

"I suppose, Poirot," I said rather diffidently, "I mustn't ask what your plans are? I've forfeited the right."

"But not at all. There is no secret about them. We return to France without delay."

"*We?*"

"Precisely—'we!' You know very well that you cannot afford to let Papa Poirot out of your sight. Eh? is it not so, my friend? But remain in England by all means if you wish—"

I shook my head. He had hit the nail on the head. I could not afford to let him out of my sight. Although I could not expect his confidence after what had happened, I could still check his actions. The only danger to Bella lay with him. Giraud and the French police were indifferent to her existence. At all costs I must keep near Poirot.

Poirot observed me attentively as these reflections passed through my mind, and gave me a nod of satisfaction.

"I am right, am I not? And as you are quite capable of trying to follow me, disguised with some absurdity such as a false beard—which everyone would perceive, *bien entendu*—I much prefer that we should voyage together. It would annoy me greatly that anyone should mock themselves at you."

"Very well, then. But it's only fair to warn you—"

"I know—I know all. You are my enemy! Be my enemy, then. It does not worry me at all."

"So long as it's all fair and aboveboard, I don't mind."

"You have to the full the English passion for 'fair play'! Now your scruples are satisfied, let us depart immediately. There is no time to be lost.

Our stay in England has been short but sufficient. I know—what I wanted to know."

The tone was light, but I read a veiled menace into the words.

"Still—" I began, and stopped.

"Still—as you say! Without doubt you are satisfied with the part you are playing. Me, I preoccupy myself with Jack Renauld."

Jack Renauld! The words gave me a start. I had completely forgotten that aspect of the case. Jack Renauld, in prison, with the shadow of the guillotine looming over him. I saw the part I was playing in a more sinister light. I could save Bella—yes, but in doing so I ran the risk of sending an innocent man to his death.

I pushed the thought from me with horror. It could not be. He would be acquitted. Certainly he would be acquitted. But the cold fear came back. Suppose he were not? What then? Could I have it on my conscience—horrible thought! Would it come to that in the end? A decision. Bella or Jack Renauld? The promptings of my heart were to save the girl I loved at any cost to myself. But, if the cost were to another, the problem was altered.

What would the girl herself say? I remembered that no word of Jack Renauld's arrest had passed my lips. As yet she was in total ignorance of the fact that her former lover was in prison charged with a hideous crime which he had not committed. When she knew, how would she act?

Would she permit her life to be saved at the expense of his? Certainly she must do nothing rash. Jack Renauld might, and probably would, be acquitted without any intervention on her part. If so, good. But if he was not! That was the terrible, the unanswerable problem. I fancied that she ran no risk of the extreme penalty. The circumstances of the crime were quite different in her case. She could plead jealousy and extreme provocation, and her youth and beauty would go for much. The fact that by a tragic mistake it was Mr. Renauld, and not his son, who paid the penalty would not alter the motive of the crime. But in any case, however lenient the sentence of the Court, it must mean a long term of imprisonment.

No, Bella must be protected. And, at the same time, Jack Renauld must be saved. How this was to be accomplished I did not see clearly. But I pinned my faith to Poirot. He *knew*. Come what might, he would manage to save an innocent man. He must find some pretext other than the real one. It might be difficult, but he would manage it somehow. And with Bella unsuspected, and Jack Renauld acquitted, all would end satisfactorily.

So I told myself repeatedly, but at the bottom of my heart there still remained a cold fear.

Twenty-four

"SAVE HIM!"

We crossed from England by the evening boat, and the following morning saw us in St. Omer, whither Jack Renauld had been taken. Poirot lost no time in visiting M. Hautet. As he did not seem disposed to make any objections to my accompanying him, I bore him company.

After various formalities and preliminaries, we were conducted to the examining magistrate's room. He greeted us cordially.

"I was told that you had returned to England, Monsieur Poirot. I am glad to find that such is not the case."

"It is true I went there, monsieur, but it was only for a flying visit. A side issue, but one that I fancied might repay investigation."

"And it did—eh?"

Poirot shrugged his shoulders. M. Hautet nodded, sighing.

"We must resign ourselves, I fear. That animal Giraud, his manners are abominable, but he is undoubtedly clever! Not much chance of that one making a mistake."

"You think not?"

It was the examining magistrate's turn to shrug his shoulders.

"Oh, well, speaking frankly—in confidence, of course—can you come to any other conclusion?"

"Frankly, there seem to me to be many points that are obscure."

"Such as—?"

But Poirot was not to be drawn.

"I have not yet tabulated them," he remarked. "It was a general reflection that I was making. I liked the young man, and should be sorry to believe him guilty of such a hideous crime. By the way, what has he to say for himself on the matter?"

The magistrate frowned.

"I cannot understand him. He seems incapable of putting up any sort of defence. It has been most difficult to get him to answer questions. He contents himself with a general denial, and beyond that takes refuge in a most obstinate silence. I am interrogating him again tomorrow, perhaps you would like to be present?"

We accepted the invitation with *empressement*.

"A distressing case," said the magistrate with a sigh. "My sympathy for Madame Renauld is profound."

"How is Madame Renauld?"

"She has not yet recovered consciousness. It is merciful in a way, poor woman, she is being spared much. The doctors say that there is no danger, but that when she comes to herself she must be kept as quiet as possible. It was, I understand, quite as much the shock as the fall which caused her present state. It would be terrible if her brain became unhinged; but I should not wonder at all—no, really, not at all."

M. Hautet leaned back, shaking his head, with a sort of mournful enjoyment, as he envisaged the gloomy prospect.

He roused himself at length, and observed with a start:

"That reminds me. I have here a letter for you, Monsieur Poirot. Let me see, where did I put it?"

He proceeded to rummage among his papers. At last he found the missive, and handed it to Poirot.

"It was sent under cover to me in order that I might forward it to you," he explained. "But as you left no address I could not do so."

Poirot studied the letter curiously. It was addressed in a long, sloping, foreign hand, and the writing was decidedly a woman's. Poirot did not open it. Instead he put it in his pocket and rose to his feet.

"Till tomorrow then. Many thanks for your courtesy and amiability."

"But not at all. I am always at your service."

We were just leaving the building when we came face to face with Giraud, looking more dandified than ever, and thoroughly pleased with himself.

"Aha! Monsieur Poirot," he cried airily. "You have returned from England then?"

"As you see," said Poirot.

"The end of the case is not far off now, I fancy."

"I agree with you, Monsieur Giraud."

Poirot spoke in a subdued tone. His crestfallen manner seemed to delight the other.

"Of all the milk-and-water criminals! Not an idea of defending himself. It is extraordinary!"

"So extraordinary that it gives one to think, does it not?" suggested Poirot mildly.

But Giraud was not even listening. He twirled his cane amicably.

"Well, good day, Monsieur Poirot. I am glad you're satisfied of young Renauld's guilt at last."

"*Pardon*! But I am not in the least satisfied. Jack Renauld is innocent."

Giraud stared for a moment—then burst out laughing, tapping his head significantly with the brief remark: "*Toqué*!"

Poirot drew himself up. A dangerous light showed in his eyes.

"Monsieur Giraud, throughout the case your manner to me has been deliberately insulting. You need teaching a lesson. I am prepared to wager you five hundred francs that I find the murderer of Monsieur Renauld before you do. Is it agreed?"

Giraud stared helplessly at him, and murmured again: "*Toqué*!"

"Come now," urged Poirot, "is it agreed?"

"I have no wish to take your money from you."

"Make your mind easy—you will not!"

"Oh, well then, I agree! You speak of my manner to you being insulting. Well, once or twice, *your* manner has annoyed *me*."

"I am enchanted to hear it," said Poirot. "Good morning, Monsieur Giraud. Come, Hastings."

I said no word as we walked along the street. My heart was heavy. Poirot had displayed his intentions only too plainly. I doubted more than ever my powers of saving Bella from the consequences of her act. This unlucky encounter with Giraud had roused Poirot and put him on his mettle.

Suddenly I felt a hand laid on my shoulder, and turned to face Gabriel Stonor. We stopped and greeted him, and he proposed strolling with us back to our hotel.

"And what are you doing here, Monsieur Stonor?" inquired Poirot.

"One must stand by one's friends," replied the other dryly. "Especially when they are unjustly accused."

"Then you do not believe that Jack Renauld committed the crime?" I asked eagerly.

"Certainly I don't. I know the lad. I admit that there have been one or two things in this business that have staggered me completely, but none the less, in spite of his fool way of taking it, I'll never believe that Jack Renauld is a murderer."

My heart warmed to the secretary. His words seemed to lift a secret weight from my heart.

"I have no doubt that many people feel as you do," I exclaimed. "There is really absurdly little evidence against him. I should say that there was no doubt of his acquittal—no doubt whatever."

But Stonor hardly responded as I could have wished.

"I'd give a lot to think as you do," he said gravely. He turned to Poirot. "What's your opinion, monsieur?"

"I think that things look very black against him," said Poirot quietly.

"You believe him guilty?" said Stonor sharply.

"No. But I think he will find it hard to prove his innocence."

"He's behaving so damned queerly," muttered Stonor. "Of course, I realize that there's a lot more in this affair than meets the eye. Giraud's not wise to that because he's an outsider, but the whole thing has been damned odd. As to that, least said soonest mended. If Mrs. Renauld wants to hush anything up, I'll take my cue from her. It's her show, and I've too much respect for her judgement to shove my oar in, but I can't get behind this attitude of Jack's. Anyone would think he *wanted* to be thought guilty."

"But it's absurd," I cried, bursting in. "For one thing, the dagger—" I paused, uncertain as to how much Poirot would wish me to reveal. I continued, choosing my words carefully, "We know that the dagger could not have been in Jack Renauld's possession that evening. Mrs. Renauld knows that."

"True," said Stonor. "When she recovers, she will doubtless say all this and more. Well, I must be leaving you."

"One moment." Poirot's hand arrested his departure. "Can you arrange for word to be sent to me at once should Mrs. Renauld recover consciousness?"

"Certainly. That's easily done."

"That point about the dagger is good, Poirot," I urged as we went upstairs. "I couldn't speak very plainly before Stonor."

"That was quite right of you. We might as well keep the knowledge to ourselves as long as we can. As to the dagger, your point hardly helps Jack Renauld. You remember that I was absent for an hour this morning, before we started from London?"

"Yes?"

"Well, I was employed in trying to find the firm Jack Renauld employed to convert his souvenirs. It was not very difficult. *Eh bien*, Hastings, they made to his order not *two* paper knives, but *three*."

"So that—"

"So that, after giving one to his mother and one to Bella Duveen, there was a third which he doubtless retained for his own use. No, Hastings,

I fear the dagger question will not help us to save him from the guillotine."

"It won't come to that," I cried, stung.

Poirot shook his head uncertainly.

"You will save him," I cried positively.

Poirot glanced at me dryly.

"Have you not rendered it impossible, *mon ami*?"

"Some other way," I muttered.

"Ah! *Sapristi*! But it is miracles you ask from me. No—say no more. Let us instead see what is in this letter."

And he drew out the envelope from his breast pocket.

His face contracted as he read, then he handed the one flimsy sheet to me.

"There are other women in the world who suffer, Hastings."

The writing was blurred and the note had evidently been written in great agitation.

> Dear M. Poirot—If you get this, I beg of you to come to my aid. I have no one to turn to, and at all costs Jack must be saved. I implore of you on my knees to help us.
>
> Marthe Daubreuil

I handed it back, moved.

"You will go?"

"At once. We will command an auto."

Half an hour later saw us at the Villa Marguerite. Marthe was at the door to meet us, and let Poirot in, clinging with both hands to one of his.

"Ah, you have come—it is good of you. I have been in despair, not knowing what to do. They will not let me go to see him in prison even. I suffer horribly. I am nearly mad.

"Is it true what they say, that he does not deny the crime? But that is madness. It is impossible that he should have done it! Never for one minute will I believe it."

"Neither do I believe it, mademoiselle," said Poirot gently.

"But then why does he not speak? I do not understand."

"Perhaps because he is screening someone," suggested Poirot, watching her.

Marthe frowned.

"Screening someone? Do you mean his mother? Ah, from the beginning I have suspected her. Who inherits all that vast fortune? She does. It is easy to wear widow's weeds and play the hypocrite. And they say that when he was arrested she fell down like *that!*" She made a dramatic gesture. "And without doubt, Monsieur Stonor, the secretary, he helped her. They are thick as thieves, those two. It is true she is older than he—but what do men care—if a woman is rich!"

There was a hint of bitterness in her tone.

"Stonor was in England," I put in.

"He says so—but who knows?"

"Mademoiselle," said Poirot quietly, "if we are to work together, you and I, we must have things clear. First, I will ask you a question."

"Yes, monsieur?"

"Are you aware of your mother's real name?"

Marthe looked at him for a minute, then, letting her head fall forward on her arms, she burst into tears.

"There, there," said Poirot, patting her on the shoulder. "Calm yourself, *petite*, I see that you know. Now a second question—did you know who Monsieur Renauld was?"

"Monsieur Renauld," she raised her head from her hands and gazed at him wonderingly.

"Ah, I see you do not know that. Now listen to me carefully."

Step by step, he went over the case, much as he had done to me on the day of our departure for England. Marthe listened spellbound. When he had finished, she drew a long breath.

"But you are wonderful—magnificent! You are the greatest detective in the world."

With a swift gesture she slipped off her chair and knelt before him with an abandonment that was wholly French.

"Save him, monsieur," she cried. "I love him so. Oh, save him, save him—save him!"

Twenty-five

AN UNEXPECTED DÉNOUEMENT

We were present the following morning at the examination of Jack Renauld. Short as the time had been, I was shocked at the change that had taken place in the young prisoner. His cheeks had fallen in, there were deep black circles round his eyes, and he looked haggard and distraught, as one who had wooed sleep in vain for several nights. He betrayed no emotion at seeing us.

"Renauld," began the magistrate, "do you deny that you were in Merlinville on the night of the crime?"

Jack did not reply at once, then he said with a hesitancy of manner which was piteous:

"I—I—told you that I was in Cherbourg."

The magistrate turned sharply.

"Send in the station witnesses."

In a moment or two the door opened to admit a man whom I recognized as being a porter at Merlinville station.

"You were on duty on the night of 7th June?"

"Yes, monsieur."

"You witnessed the arrival of the 11:40 train?"

"Yes, monsieur."

"Look at the prisoner. Do you recognize him as having been one of the passengers to alight?"

"Yes, monsieur."

"There is no possibility of your being mistaken?"

"No, monsieur. I know Monsieur Jack Renauld well."

"Nor of your being mistaken as to the date?"

"No, monsieur. Because it was the following morning, 8th June, that we heard of the murder."

Another railway official was brought in, and confirmed the first one's evidence. The magistrate looked at Jack Renauld.

"These men have identified you positively. What have you to say?"

Jack shrugged his shoulders.

"Nothing."

"Renauld," continued the magistrate, "do you recognize this?"

He took something from the table by his side and held it out to the prisoner. I shuddered as I recognized the aeroplane dagger.

"Pardon," cried Jack's counsel, Maître Grosier. "I demand to speak to my client before he answers that question."

But Jack Renauld had no consideration for the feelings of the wretched Grosier. He waved him aside, and replied quietly:

"Certainly I recognize it. It was a present given by me to my mother, as a souvenir of the war."

"Is there, as far as you know, any duplicate of that dagger in existence?"

Again Maître Grosier burst out, and again Jack overrode him.

"Not that I know of. The setting was my own design."

Even the magistrate almost gasped at the boldness of the reply. It did, in very truth, seem as though Jack was rushing on his fate. I realized, of course, the vital necessity he was under of concealing, for Bella's sake, the fact that there was a duplicate dagger in the case. So long as there was supposed to be only one weapon, no suspicion was likely to attach to the girl who had had the second paper knife in her possession. He was valiantly shielding the woman he had once loved—but at what cost to himself! I began to realize the magnitude of the task I had so lightly set Poirot. It would not be easy to secure the acquittal of Jack Renauld by anything short of the truth.

M. Hautet spoke again, with a peculiarly biting inflection:

"Madame Renauld told us that this dagger was on her dressing table on the night of the crime. But Madame Renauld is a mother! It will doubtless astonish you, Renauld, but I consider it highly likely that Madame Renauld was mistaken, and that, by inadvertence perhaps, you had taken it with you to Paris. Doubtless you will contradict me—"

I saw the lad's handcuffed hands clench

themselves. The perspiration stood out in beads upon his brow, as with a supreme effort he interrupted M. Hautet in a hoarse voice:

"I shall not contradict you. It is possible."

It was a stupefying moment. Maître Grosier rose to his feet, protesting:

"My client has undergone a considerable nervous strain. I should wish it put on record that I do not consider him answerable for what he says."

The magistrate quelled him angrily. For a moment a doubt seemed to arise in his own mind. Jack Renauld had almost overdone his part. He leaned forward, and gazed at the prisoner searchingly.

"Do you fully understand, Renauld, that on the answers you have given me I shall have no alternative but to commit you for trial?"

Jack's pale face flushed. He looked steadily back.

"Monsieur Hautet, I swear that I did not kill my father."

But the magistrate's brief moment of doubt was over. He laughed a short unpleasant laugh.

"Without doubt, without doubt—they are always innocent, our prisoners! By your own mouth you are condemned. You can offer no defence, no alibi—only a mere assertion which would not deceive a babe!—that you are not guilty. You killed your father, Renauld—a cruel and cowardly murder—for the sake of the money which you believed would come to you at his death. Your mother was an accessory after the fact. Doubtless, in view of the fact that she acted as a mother, the courts will extend an indulgence to her that they will not accord to you. And rightly so! Your crime was a horrible one—to be held in abhorrence by gods and men!"

M. Hautet was interrupted—to his intense annoyance. The door was pushed open.

"Monsieur le juge, Monsieur le juge," stammered the attendant, "there is a lady who says—who says—"

"Who says what?" cried the justly incensed magistrate. "This is highly irregular. I forbid it— I absolutely forbid it."

But a slender figure pushed the stammering gendarme aside. Dressed all in black, with a long veil that hid her face, she advanced into the room.

My heart gave a sickening throb. She had come then! All my efforts were in vain. Yet I could not but admire the courage that had led her to take this step so unfalteringly.

She raised her veil—and I gasped. For, though as like her as two peas, this girl was not Cinderella! On the other hand, now that I saw her without the fair wig she had worn on the stage, I recognized her as the girl of the photograph in Jack Renauld's room.

"You are the Juge d'Instruction, Monsieur Hautet?" she queried.

"Yes, but I forbid—"

"My name is Bella Duveen. I wish to give myself up for the murder of Mr. Renauld."

Twenty-six

I Receive a Letter

"My friend,—You will know all when you get this. Nothing that I can say will move Bella. She has gone out to give herself up. I am tired out with struggling.

"You will know now that I deceived you, that where you gave me trust I repaid you with lies. It will seem, perhaps, indefensible to you, but I should like, before I go out of your life for ever, to show you just how it all came about. If I knew that you forgave me, it would make life easier for me. It wasn't for myself I did it—that's the only thing I can put forward to say for myself.

"I'll begin from the day I met you in the boat train from Paris. I was uneasy then about Bella. She was just desperate about Jack Renauld, she'd have lain down on the ground for him to walk on, and when he began to change, and to stop writing so often, she began getting in a state. She got it into her head that he was keen on another girl—and of course, as it turned out afterwards, she was quite right there. She'd made up her mind to go to their villa at Merlinville, and try and see Jack. She knew I was against it, and tried to give me the slip. I found she was not on the train at Calais, and determined I would not go on to England without her. I'd an uneasy feeling that something awful was going to happen if I couldn't prevent it.

"I met the next train from Paris. She was on it, and set upon going out then and there to Merlinville. I argued with her for all I was worth, but it wasn't any good. She was all strung up and set upon having her own way. Well, I washed my hands of it. I'd done all I could. It was getting late. I went to an hotel, and Bella started for Merlinville. I still couldn't shake off my feeling of what the books call 'impending disaster.'

"The next day came—but no Bella. She'd made a date with me to meet at the hotel, but she didn't keep it. No sign of her all day. I got more and more anxious. Then came an evening paper with the news.

"It was awful! I couldn't be sure, of course—but I was terribly afraid. I figured it out that Bella had met Papa Renauld and told him about her and Jack, and that he'd insulted her or something like that. We've both got terribly quick tempers.

"Then all the masked foreigner business came out, and I began to feel more at ease. But it still worried me that Bella hadn't kept her date with me.

"By the next morning I was so rattled that I'd just got to go and see what I could. First thing, I ran up against you. You know all that . . . When I saw the dead man, looking so like Jack, and wearing Jack's fancy overcoat, I knew! And there was the identical paper knife—wicked little thing!—that Jack had given Bella! Ten to one it had her fingermarks on it. I can't hope to explain to you the sort of helpless horror of that moment. I only saw one thing clearly—I must get hold of that dagger, and get right away with it before they found out it was gone. I pretended to faint, and while you were away getting water I took the thing and hid it away in my dress.

"I told you that I was staying at the Hôtel du Phare, but of course really I made a beeline back to Calais, and then on to England by the first boat. When we were in mid-Channel I dropped that little devil of a dagger into the sea. Then I felt I could breathe again.

"Bella was in our digs in London. She looked like nothing on God's earth. I told her what I'd done, and that she was pretty safe for the time being. She stared at me, and then began laughing . . . laughing . . . laughing . . . it was horrible to hear her! I felt that the best thing to do was to keep busy. She'd go mad if she had time to brood on what she'd done. Luckily we got an engagement at once.

"And then, I saw you and your friend watching

us that night . . . I was frantic. You must suspect, or you wouldn't have tracked us down. I had to know the worst, so I followed you. I was desperate. And then, before I'd had time to say anything, I tumbled to it that it was me you suspected, not Bella! Or at least that you thought I *was* Bella, since I'd stolen the dagger.

"I wish, honey, that you could see back into my mind at that moment . . . you'd forgive me, perhaps . . . I was so frightened, and muddled, and desperate . . . All I could get clearly was that you would try and save me—I didn't know whether you'd be willing to save her . . . I thought very likely not—It wasn't the same thing! And I couldn't risk it! Bella's my twin—I'd got to do the best for her. So I went on lying. I felt mean—I feel mean still . . . That's all—enough too, you'll say, I expect. I ought to have trusted you . . . If I had—

"As soon as the news was in the paper that Jack Renauld had been arrested, it was all up. Bella wouldn't even wait to see how things went. . . .

"I'm very tired. I can't write any more."

She had begun to sign herself Cinderella, but had crossed that out and written instead "Dulcie Duveen."

It was an ill-written, blurred epistle—but I have kept it to this day.

Poirot was with me when I read it. The sheets fell from my hand, and I looked across at him.

"Did you know all the time that it was—the other?"

"Yes, my friend."

"Why did you not tell me?"

"To begin with, I could hardly believe it conceivable that you could make such a mistake. You had seen the photograph. The sisters are very alike, but by no means incapable of distinguishment."

"But the fair hair?"

"A wig, worn for the sake of a piquant contrast on the stage. Is it conceivable that with twins one should be fair and one dark?"

"Why didn't you tell me that night at the hotel in Coventry?"

"You were rather high-handed in your methods, *mon ami*," said Poirot dryly. "You did not give me a chance."

"But afterwards?"

"Ah, afterwards! Well, to begin with, I was hurt at your want of faith in me. And then, I wanted to see whether your—feelings would stand the test of time. In fact, whether it was love, or a flash in the pan, with you. I should not have left you long in your error."

I nodded. His tone was too affectionate for me to bear resentment. I looked down on the sheets of the letter. Suddenly I picked them up from the floor, and pushed them across to him.

"Read that," I said. "I'd like you to."

He read it through in silence, then he looked up at me.

"What is it that worries you, Hastings?"

This was quite a new mood in Poirot. His mocking manner seemed laid quite aside. I was able to say what I wanted without too much difficulty.

"She doesn't say—she doesn't say—well, not whether she cares for me or not?"

Poirot turned back the pages.

"I think you are mistaken, Hastings."

"Where?" I cried, leaning forward eagerly.

Poirot smiled.

"She tells you that in every line of the letter, *mon ami*."

"But where am I to find her? There's no address on the letter. There's a French stamp, that's all."

"Excite yourself not! Leave it to Papa Poirot. I can find her for you as soon as I have five little minutes!"

Twenty-seven

JACK RENAULD'S STORY

"Congratulations, Monsieur Jack," said Poirot, wringing the lad warmly by the hand.

Young Renauld had come to us as soon as he was liberated—before starting for Merlinville to rejoin Marthe and his mother. Stonor accompanied him.

His heartiness was in strong contrast to the lad's wan looks. It was plain that the boy was on the verge of a nervous breakdown. He smiled mournfully at Poirot, and said in a low voice:

"I went through it to protect her, and now it's all no use."

"You could hardly expect the girl to accept the price of your life," remarked Stonor dryly. "She was bound to come forward when she saw you heading straight for the guillotine."

"*Eh ma foi*! and you were heading for it too!" added Poirot, with a slight twinkle. "You would have had Maître Grosier's death from rage on your conscience if you had gone on."

"He was a well-meaning ass, I suppose," said Jack. "But he worried me horribly. You see, I couldn't very well take him into my confidence. But, my God! what's going to happen about Bella?"

"If I were you," said Poirot frankly, "I should not distress myself unduly. The French Courts are very lenient to youth and beauty, and the *crime passionnel*! A clever lawyer will make out a great case of extenuating circumstances. It will not be pleasant for you—"

"I don't care about that. You see, Monsieur Poirot, in a way I *do* feel guilty of my father's murder. But for me, and my entanglement with this girl, he would be alive and well today. And then my cursed carelessness in taking away the wrong overcoat. I can't help feeling responsible for his death. It will haunt me for ever!"

"No, no," I said soothingly.

"Of course it's horrible to me to think that Bella killed my father," resumed Jack. "But I'd treated her shamefully. After I met Marthe, and realized I'd made a mistake, I ought to have written and told her so honestly. But I was so terrified of a row, and of its coming to Marthe's ears, and her thinking there was more in it than there ever had been, that—well, I was a coward, and went on hoping the thing would die down of itself. I just drifted, in fact—not realizing that I was driving the poor kid desperate. If she'd really knifed me, as she meant to, I should have got no more than my deserts. And the way she's come forward now is downright plucky. I'd have stood the racket, you know—up to the end."

He was silent for a moment or two, and then burst out on another tack:

"What gets me is why the Governor should be wandering about in underclothes and my overcoat at that time of night. I suppose he'd just given the foreign johnnies the slip, and my mother must have made a mistake about its being two o'clock when they came. Or—or, it wasn't all a frame-up, was it? I mean, my mother didn't think—couldn't think—that—that it was *me?*"

Poirot reassured him quickly.

"No, no, Monsieur Jack. Have no fears on that score. As for the rest, I will explain it to you one of these days. It is rather curious. But will you recount to us exactly what did occur on that terrible evening?"

"There's very little to tell. I came from Cherbourg, as I told you, in order to see Marthe before going to the other end of the world. The train was late, and I decided to take the short cut across the golf links. I could easily get into the grounds of the Villa Marguerite from there. I had nearly reached the place when—"

He paused and swallowed.

"Yes?"

"I heard a terrible cry. It wasn't loud—a sort of choke and gasp—but it frightened me. For a moment I stood rooted to the spot. Then I came round the corner of a bush. There was moonlight. I saw the grave, and a figure lying face downwards with a dagger sticking in the back. And then—and then—I looked up and saw *her*. She was looking at me as though she saw a ghost—it's what she must have thought me at first—all expression seemed frozen out of her face by horror. And then she gave a cry, and turned and ran."

He stopped, trying to master his emotion.

"And afterwards?" asked Poirot gently.

"I really don't know. I stayed there for a time, dazed. And then I realized I'd better get away as fast as I could. It didn't occur to me that they would suspect me, but I was afraid of being called upon to give evidence against her. I walked to St. Beauvais as I told you, and got a car from there back to Cherbourg."

A knock came at the door, and a page entered with a telegram which he delivered to Stonor. He tore it open. Then he got up from his seat.

"Mrs. Renauld has regained consciousness," he said.

"Ah!" Poirot sprang to his feet. "Let us all go to Merlinville at once!"

A hurried departure was made forthwith. Stonor, at Jack's insistence, agreed to stay behind and do all that could be done for Bella Duveen. Poirot, Jack Renauld, and I set off in the Renauld car.

The run took just over forty minutes. As we approached the doorway of the Villa Marguerite Jack Renauld shot a questioning glance at Poirot.

"How would it be if you went on first—to break the news to my mother that I am free—"

"While you break it in person to Mademoiselle Marthe, eh?" finished Poirot, with a twinkle. "But yes, by all means, I was about to propose such an arrangement myself."

Jack Renauld did not wait for more. Stopping the car, he swung himself out, and ran up the path to the front door. We went on in the car to the Villa Geneviève.

"Poirot," I said, "do you remember how we arrived here that first day? And were met by the news of Mr. Renauld's murder?"

"Ah, yes, truly. Not so long ago either. But what a lot of things have happened since then—especially for *you, mon ami!*"

"Yes, indeed," I sighed.

"You are regarding it from the sentimental standpoint, Hastings. That was not my meaning. We will hope that Mademoiselle Bella will be dealt with leniently, and after all Jack Renauld cannot marry both the girls! I spoke from a professional standpoint. This is not a crime well-ordered and regular, such as a detective delights in. The *mise en scène* designed by Georges Conneau, that indeed is perfect, but the *dénouement*—ah, no! A man killed by accident in a girl's fit of anger—ah, indeed, what order or method is there in that?"

And in the midst of a fit of laughter on my part at Poirot's peculiarities, the door was opened by Françoise.

Poirot explained that he must see Mrs. Renauld at once, and the old woman conducted him upstairs. I remained in the salon. It was some time before Poirot reappeared. He was looking unusually grave.

"*Vous voilà*, Hastings! *Sacré tonnerre*! but there are squalls ahead!"

"What do you mean?" I cried.

"I would hardly have credited it," said Poirot thoughtfully, "but women are very unexpected."

"Here are Jack and Marthe Daubreuil," I exclaimed, looking out of the window.

Poirot bounded out of the room, and met the young couple on the steps outside.

"Do not enter. It is better not. Your mother is very upset."

"I know, I know," said Jack Renauld. "I must go up to her at once."

"But no, I tell you. It is better not."

"But Marthe and I—"

"In any case, do not take Mademoiselle with you. Mount, if you must, but you would be wise to be guided by me."

A voice on the stairs behind made us all start.

"I thank you for your good offices, Monsieur Poirot, but I will make my own wishes clear."

We stared in astonishment. Descending the stairs, leaning on Léonie's arm, was Mrs. Renauld, her head still bandaged. The French girl was weeping, and imploring her mistress to return to bed.

"Madame will kill herself. It is contrary to all the doctor's orders!"

But Mrs. Renauld came on.

"Mother," cried Jack, starting forward.

But with a gesture she drove him back.

"I am no mother of yours! You are no son of mine! From this day and hour I renounce you."

"Mother!" cried the lad, stupefied.

For a moment she seemed to waver, to falter before the anguish in his voice. Poirot made a mediating gesture. But instantly she regained command of herself.

"Your father's blood is on your head. You are morally guilty of his death. You thwarted and defied him over this girl, and by your heartless treatment of another girl, you brought about his death. Go out from my house. Tomorrow I intend to take such steps as shall make it certain that you shall never touch a penny of his money. Make your way in the world as best you can with the help of the girl who is the daughter of your father's bitterest enemy!"

And slowly, painfully, she retraced her way upstairs.

We were all dumbfounded—totally unprepared for such a demonstration. Jack Renauld, worn out with all he had already gone through, swayed and nearly fell. Poirot and I went quickly to his assistance.

"He is overdone," murmured Poirot to Marthe. "Where can we take him?"

"But home! To the Villa Marguerite. We will nurse him, my mother and I. My poor Jack!"

We got the lad to the villa, where he dropped limply on to a chair in a semi-dazed condition. Poirot felt his head and hands.

"He has fever. The long strain begins to tell.

And now this shock on top of it. Get him to bed, and Hastings and I will summon a doctor."

A doctor was soon procured. After examining the patient, he gave it as his opinion that it was simply a case of nerve strain. With perfect rest and quiet, the lad might be almost restored by the next day, but, if excited, there was a chance of brain fever. It would be advisable for someone to sit up all night with him.

Finally, having done all we could, we left him in the charge of Marthe and her mother, and set out for the town. It was past our usual hour of dining, and we were both famished. The first restaurant we came to assuaged the pangs of hunger with an excellent omelette, and an equally excellent entrecôte to follow.

"And now for quarters for the night," said Poirot, when at length *café noir* had completed the meal. "Shall we try our old friend, the Hôtel de Bains?"

We traced our steps there without more ado. Yes, Messieurs could be accommodated with two good rooms overlooking the sea. Then Poirot asked a question which surprised me:

"Has an English lady, Miss Robinson, arrived?"

"Yes, Monsieur. She is in the little salon."

"Ah!"

"Poirot," I cried, keeping pace with him, as he walked along the corridor, "who on earth is Miss Robinson?"

Poirot beamed kindly on me.

"It is that I have arranged you a marriage, Hastings."

"But I say—"

"Bah!" said Poirot, giving me a friendly push over the threshold of the door. "Do you think I wish to trumpet aloud in Merlinville the name of Duveen?"

It was indeed Cinderella who rose to greet us. I took her hand in both of mine. My eyes said the rest.

Poirot cleared his throat.

"*Mes enfants*," he said, "for the moment we have no time for sentiment. There is work ahead of us. Mademoiselle, were you able to do what I asked you?"

In response, Cinderella took from her bag an object wrapped up in paper, and handed it silently to Poirot. The latter unwrapped it. I gave a start— for it was the aeroplane dagger which I understood she had cast into the sea. Strange, how reluctant women always are to destroy the most compromising of objects and documents!

"*Très bien, mon enfant*," said Poirot. "I am pleased with you. Go now and rest yourself. Hastings here and I have work to do. You shall see him tomorrow."

"Where are you going?" asked the girl, her eyes widening.

"You shall hear all about it tomorrow."

"Because wherever you're going, I'm coming too."

"But, mademoiselle—"

"I'm coming too, I tell you."

Poirot realized that it was futile to argue. He gave in.

"Come then, mademoiselle. But it will not be amusing. In all probability nothing will happen."

The girl made no reply.

Twenty minutes later we set forth. It was quite dark now, a close oppressive evening. Poirot led the way out of the town in the direction of the Villa Geneviève. But when he reached the Villa Marguerite he paused.

"I should like to assure myself that all goes well with Jack Renauld. Come with me, Hastings. Mademoiselle will perhaps remain outside. Madame Daubreuil might say something which would wound her."

We unlatched the gate, and walked up the path. As we went round to the side of the house, I drew Poirot's attention to a window on the first floor. Thrown sharply on the blind was the profile of Marthe Daubreuil.

"Ah!" said Poirot. "I figure to myself that that is the room where we shall find Jack Renauld."

Madame Daubreuil opened the door to us. She explained that Jack was much the same, but perhaps we would like to see for ourselves. She led us upstairs and into the bedroom. Marthe Daubreuil was sitting by a table with a lamp on it, working. She put her finger to her lips as we entered.

Jack Renauld was sleeping an uneasy, fitful sleep, his head turning from side to side, and his face still unduly flushed.

"Is the doctor coming again?" asked Poirot in a whisper.

"Not unless we send. He is sleeping—that is the great thing. *Maman* made him a tisane."

She sat down again with her embroidery as we left the room. Madame Daubreuil accompanied us down the stairs. Since I had learned of her past history, I viewed this woman with increased interest. She stood there with her eyes cast down, the same very faint enigmatical smile that I remembered on her lips. And suddenly I felt afraid of her, as one might feel afraid of a beautiful poisonous snake.

"I hope we have not deranged you, madame," said Poirot politely, as she opened the door for us to pass out.

"Not at all, monsieur."

"By the way," said Poirot, as though struck by an afterthought, "Monsieur Stonor has not been in Merlinville today, has he?"

I could not at all fathom the point of this question, which I well knew to be meaningless as far as Poirot was concerned.

Madame Daubreuil replied quite composedly:

"Not that I know of."

"He has not had an interview with Madame Renauld?"

"How should I know that, monsieur?"

"True," said Poirot. "I thought you might have seen him coming or going, that is all. Goodnight, madame."

"Why—" I began.

"No whys, Hastings. There will be time for that later."

We rejoined Cinderella and made our way rapidly in the direction of the Villa Geneviève. Poirot looked over his shoulder once at the lighted window and the profile of Marthe as she bent over her work.

"He is being guarded at all events," he muttered.

Arrived at the Villa Geneviève, Poirot took up his stand behind some bushes to the left of the drive, where, while enjoying a good view ourselves, we were completely hidden from sight. The villa itself was in total darkness, everybody was without doubt in bed and asleep. We were almost immediately under the window of Mrs. Renauld's bedroom, which window, I noticed, was open. It seemed to me that it was upon this spot that Poirot's eyes were fixed.

"What are we going to do?" I whispered.

"Watch."

"But—"

"I do not expect anything to happen for at least an hour, probably two hours, but the—"

His words were interrupted by a long, thin drawn cry:

"Help!"

A light flashed up in the first-floor room on the right-hand side of the front door. The cry came from there. And even as we watched there came a shadow on the blind as of two people struggling.

"*Mille tonnerres!*" cried Poirot. "She must have changed her room."

Dashing forward, he battered wildly on the front door. Then rushing to the tree in the flower bed, he swarmed up it with the agility of a cat. I followed him, as with a bound he sprang in through the open window. Looking over my shoulder, I saw Dulcie reaching the branch behind me.

"Take care," I exclaimed.

"Take care of your grandmother!" retorted the girl. "This is child's play to me."

Poirot had rushed through the empty room and was pounding on the door.

"Locked and bolted on the outside," he growled. "And it will take time to burst it open."

The cries for help were getting noticeably fainter. I saw despair in Poirot's eyes. He and I together put our shoulders to the door.

Cinderella's voice, calm and dispassionate, came from the window:

"You'll be too late. I guess I'm the only one who can do anything."

Before I could move a hand to stop her, she appeared to leap from the window into space. I rushed and looked out. To my horror, I saw her hanging by her hands from the roof, propelling herself along by jerks in the direction of the lighted window.

"Good heavens! She'll be killed," I cried.

"You forget. She's a professional acrobat, Hastings. It was the providence of the good God that made her insist on coming with us tonight. I only pray that she may be in time. Ah!"

A cry of absolute terror floated out on to the night, as the girl disappeared through the window, and then in Cinderella's clear tones came the words:

"No, you don't! I've got you—and my wrists are just like steel."

At the same moment the door of our prison was opened cautiously by Françoise. Poirot brushed her aside unceremoniously and rushed down the passage to where the other maids were grouped round the farther door.

"It's locked on the inside, monsieur."

There was the sound of a heavy fall within. After a moment or two the key turned and the door swung slowly open. Cinderella, very pale, beckoned us in.

"She is safe?" demanded Poirot.

"Yes, I was just in time. She was exhausted."

Mrs. Renauld was half sitting, half lying on the bed. She was gasping for breath.

"Nearly strangled me," she murmured painfully.

The girl picked up something from the floor and handed it to Poirot. It was a rolled-up ladder of silk rope, very fine but quite strong.

"A getaway," said Poirot. "By the window, while we were battering at the door. Where is—the other?"

The girl stood aside a little and pointed. On the ground lay a figure wrapped in some dark material, a fold of which hid the face.

"Dead?"

She nodded.

"I think so. Head must have struck the marble fender."

"But who is it?" I cried.

"The murderer of Renauld, Hastings. And the would-be murderer of Madame Renauld."

Puzzled and uncomprehending, I knelt down, and lifting the fold of cloth, looked into the dead beautiful face of Marthe Daubreuil!

Twenty-eight

JOURNEY'S END

I have confused memories of the further events of that night. Poirot seemed deaf to my repeated questions. He was engaged in overwhelming Françoise with reproaches for not having told him of Mrs. Renauld's change of sleeping quarters.

I caught him by the shoulder, determined to attract his attention, and make myself heard.

"But you *must* have known," I expostulated. "You were taken up to see her this afternoon."

Poirot deigned to attend to me for a brief moment.

"She had been wheeled on a sofa into the middle room—her boudoir," he explained.

"But, monsieur," cried Françoise, "Madame changed her room almost immediately after the crimes. The associations—they were too distressing!"

"Then why was I not told?" vociferated Poirot, striking the table, and working himself into a first-class passion. "I demand of you—why—was—I—not—told? You are an old woman completely imbecile! And Léonie and Denise are no better. All of you are triple idiots! Your stupidity has nearly caused the death of your mistress. But for this courageous child—"

He broke off, and, darting across the room to where the girl was bending over ministering to Mrs. Renauld, he embraced her with Gallic fervour—slightly to my annoyance.

I was aroused from my condition of mental fog by a sharp command from Poirot to fetch the doctor immediately on Mrs. Renauld's behalf. After that, I might summon the police. And he added, to complete my dudgeon:

"It will hardly be worth your while to return

273

here. I shall be too busy to attend to you, and of Mademoiselle here I make a *garde-malade*."

I retired with what dignity I could command. Having done my errands, I returned to the hotel. I understood next to nothing of what had occurred. The events of the night seemed fantastic and impossible. Nobody would answer my questions. Nobody had seemed to hear them. Angrily, I flung myself into bed, and slept the sleep of the bewildered and utterly exhausted.

I awoke to find the sun pouring in through the open windows and Poirot, neat and smiling, sitting beside the bed.

"*Enfin*, you wake! But it is that you are a famous sleeper, Hastings! Do you know that it is nearly eleven o'clock?"

I groaned and put a hand to my head.

"I must have been dreaming," I said. "Do you know, I actually dreamt that we found Marthe Daubreuil's body in Mrs. Renauld's room, and that you declared her to have murdered Mr. Renauld?"

"You were not dreaming. All that is quite true."

"But Bella Duveen killed Mr. Renauld?"

"Oh no, Hastings, she did not! She said she did—yes—but that was to save the man she loved from the guillotine."

"What?"

"Remember Jack Renauld's story. They both arrived on the scene on the same instant, and each took the other to be the perpetrator of the crime. The girl stares at him in horror, and then with a cry rushes away. But, when she hears that the crime has been brought home to him, she cannot bear it, and comes forward to accuse herself and save him from certain death."

Poirot leaned back in his chair, and brought the tips of his fingers together in familiar style.

"The case was not quite satisfactory to me," he observed judicially. "All along I was strongly under the impression that we were dealing with a cold-blooded and premeditated crime committed by someone who had contented themselves (very cleverly) with using Monsieur Renauld's own plans for throwing the police off the track. The great criminal (as you may remember my remarking to you once) is always supremely simple."

I nodded.

"Now, to support this theory, the criminal must have been fully cognizant of Monsieur Renauld's plans. That leads us to Mrs. Renauld. But facts fail to support any theory of her guilt. Is there anyone else who might have known of them? Yes. From Marthe Daubreuil's own lips we have the admission that she overheard Mr. Renauld's quarrel with the tramp. If she could overhear that, there is no reason why she should not have heard everything else, especially if Mr. and Madame Renauld were imprudent enough to discuss their plans sitting on the bench. Remember how easily you overheard Marthe's conversation with Jack Renauld from that spot."

"But what possible motive could Marthe have for murdering Mr. Renauld?" I argued.

"What motive! Money! Renauld was a millionaire several times over, and at his death (or so she and Jack believed) half that vast fortune would pass to his son. Let us reconstruct the scene from the standpoint of Marthe Daubreuil.

"Marthe Daubreuil overhears what passes between Renauld and his wife. So far he has been a nice little source of income to the Daubreuil mother and daughter, but now he proposes to escape from their toils. At first, possibly, her idea is to prevent that escape. But a bolder idea takes its place, and one that fails to horrify the daughter of Jeanne Beroldy! At present Renauld stands inexorably in the way of her marriage with Jack. If the latter defies his father, he will be a pauper—which is not at all to the mind of Mademoiselle Marthe. In fact, I doubt if she has ever cared a straw for Jack Renauld. She can simulate emotion but in reality she is of the same cold, calculating type as her mother. I doubt, too, whether she was really very sure of her hold over the boy's affections. She had dazzled and captivated him, but separated from her, as his father could so easily manage to separate him, she might lose him. But with Renauld dead, and

Jack the heir to half his millions, the marriage can take place at once, and at a stroke she will attain wealth—not the beggarly thousands that have been extracted from him so far. And her clever brain takes in the simplicity of the thing. It is all so easy. Renauld is planning all the circumstances of his death—she has only to step in at the right moment and turn the farce into a grim reality. And here comes in the second point which led me infallibly to Marthe Daubreuil—the dagger! Jack Renauld had *three* souvenirs made. One he gave to his mother, one to Bella Duveen—was it not highly probable that he had given the third one to Marthe Daubreuil?

"So, then, to sum up, there were four points of note against Marthe Daubreuil:

1. Marthe Daubreuil could have overheard Renauld's plans.
2. Marthe Daubreuil had a direct interest in causing Renauld's death.
3. Marthe Daubreuil was the daughter of the notorious Madame Beroldy who in my opinion was morally and virtually the murderess of her husband, although it may have been Georges Conneau's hand which struck the actual blow.
4. Marthe Daubreuil was the only person, besides Jack Renauld, likely to have the third dagger in her possession."

Poirot paused and cleared his throat.

"Of course, when I learned of the existence of the other girl, Bella Duveen, I realized that it was quite possible that *she* might have killed Renauld. The solution did not commend itself to me, because, as I pointed out to you, Hastings, an expert, such as I am, likes to meet a foeman worthy of his steel. Still, one must take crimes as one finds them, not as one would like them to be. It did not seem very likely that Bella Duveen would be wandering about carrying a souvenir paper knife in her hand, but of course she might have had some idea all the time of revenging herself on Jack Renauld. When she actually came forward and confessed to the murder, it seemed that all was over. And yet—I was not satisfied, *mon ami. I was not satisfied.* . . .

"I went over the case again minutely, and I came to the same conclusion as before. If it was *not* Bella Duveen, the only other person who could have committed the crime was Marthe Daubreuil. But I had not one single proof against her!

"And then you showed me that letter from Mademoiselle Dulcie, and I saw a chance of settling the matter once for all. The original dagger was stolen by Dulcie Duveen and thrown into the sea—since, as she thought, it belonged to her sister. But if, by any chance, it was *not* her sister's, but the one given by Jack to Marthe

Daubreuil—why then, Bella Duveen's dagger would be still intact! I said no word to you, Hastings (it was no time for romance), but I sought out Mademoiselle Dulcie, told her as much as I deemed needful, and set her to search among the effects of her sister. Imagine my elation, when she sought me out (according to my instructions) as Miss Robinson, with the precious souvenir in her possession!

"In the meantime I had taken steps to force Mademoiselle Marthe into the open. By my orders, Madame Renauld repulsed her son, and declared her intention of making a will on the morrow which should cut him off from ever enjoying even a portion of his father's fortune. It was a desperate step, but a necessary one, and Madame Renauld was fully prepared to take the risk—though unfortunately she also never thought of mentioning her change of room. I suppose she took it for granted that I knew. All happened as I thought. Marthe Daubreuil made a last bold bid for the Renauld millions—and failed!"

"What absolutely bewilders me," I said, "is how she ever got into the house without our seeing her. It seems an absolute miracle. We left her behind at the Villa Marguerite, we go straight to the Villa Geneviève—and yet she is there before us!"

"Ah, but we did not leave her behind. She was

out of the Villa Marguerite by the back way while we were talking to her mother in the hall. That is where, as the Americans say, she 'put it over' on Hercule Poirot!"

"But the shadow on the blind? We saw it from the road."

"*Eh bien*, when we looked up, Madame Daubreuil had just had time to run upstairs and take her place."

"Madame Daubreuil?"

"Yes. One is old, and one is young, one dark, and one fair, but, for the purpose of a silhouette on a blind, their profiles are singularly alike. Even I did not suspect—triple imbecile that I was! I thought I had plenty of time before me— that she would not try to gain admission to the villa until much later. She had brains, that beautiful Mademoiselle Marthe."

"And her object was to murder Mrs. Renauld?"

"Yes. The whole fortune would then pass to her son. But it would have been suicide, *mon ami*! On the floor by Marthe Daubreuil's body, I found a pad and a little bottle of chloroform and a hypodermic syringe containing a fatal dose of morphine. You understand? The chloroform first—then when the victim is unconscious the prick of the needle. By the morning the smell of the chloroform has quite disappeared, and the syringe lies where it has fallen from Madame Renauld's hand. What would he say, the excellent

Monsieur Hautet? 'Poor woman! What did I tell you? The shock of joy, it was too much on top of the rest! Did I not say that I should not be surprised if her brain became unhinged. Altogether a most tragic case, the Renauld Case!'

"However, Hastings, things did not go quite as Mademoiselle Marthe had planned. To begin with, Madame Renauld was awake and waiting for her. There is a struggle. But Madame Renauld is terribly weak still. There is a last chance for Marthe Daubreuil. The idea of suicide is at an end, but if she can silence Madame Renauld with her strong hands, make a getaway with her little silk ladder while we are still battering on the inside of the farther door, and be back at the Villa Marguerite before we return there, it will be hard to prove anything against her. But she was checkmated, not by Hercule Poirot, but by *la petite acrobate* with her wrists of steel."

I mused over the whole story.

"When did you first begin to suspect Marthe Daubreuil, Poirot? When she told us she had overheard the quarrel in the garden?"

Poirot smiled.

"My friend, do you remember when we drove into Merlinville that first day? And the beautiful girl we saw standing at the gate? You asked me if I had noticed a young goddess, and I replied to you that I had seen only a girl with anxious eyes. That is how I have thought of Marthe Daubreuil from the beginning. *The girl with the anxious eyes!* Why was she anxious? Not on Jack Renauld's behalf, for she did not know then that he had been in Merlinville the previous evening."

"By the way," I exclaimed, "how is Jack Renauld?"

"Much better. He is still at the Villa Marguerite. But Madame Daubreuil has disappeared. The police are looking for her."

"Was she in with her daughter, do you think?"

"We shall never know. Madame is a lady who can keep her secrets. And I doubt very much if the police will ever find her."

"Has Jack Renauld been—told?"

"Not yet."

"It will be a terrible shock to him."

"Naturally. And yet, do you know, Hastings, I doubt if his heart was ever seriously engaged? So far we have looked upon Bella Duveen as a siren, and Marthe Daubreuil as the girl he really loved. But I think that if we reversed the terms we should come nearer to the truth. Marthe Daubreuil was very beautiful. She set herself to fascinate Jack, and she succeeded, but remember his curious reluctance to break with the other girl. And see how he was willing to go to the guillotine rather than implicate her. I have a little idea that when he learns the truth, he will be horrified—revolted, and his false love will wither away."

"What about Giraud?"

"He has a *crise* of the nerves, that one! He has been obliged to return to Paris."

We both smiled.

Poirot proved a fairly true prophet. When at length the doctor pronounced Jack Renauld strong enough to hear the truth, it was Poirot who broke it to him. The shock was indeed terrific. Yet Jack rallied better than I could have supposed possible. His mother's devotion helped him to live through those difficult days. The mother and son were inseparable now.

There was a further revelation to come. Poirot had acquainted Mrs. Renauld with the fact that he knew her secret, and had represented to her that Jack should not be left in ignorance of his father's past.

"To hide the truth, never does it avail, madame! Be brave and tell him everything."

With a heavy heart Mrs. Renauld consented, and her son learned that the father he had loved had been in actual fact a fugitive from justice. A halting question was promptly answered by Poirot.

"Reassure yourself, Monsieur Jack. The world knows nothing. As far as I can see, there is no obligation for me to take the police into my confidence. Throughout the case I have acted, not for them, but for your father. Justice overtook him at last, but no one need ever know that he and Georges Conneau were one and the same."

There were, of course, various points in the case that remained puzzling to the police, but Poirot explained things in so plausible a fashion that all query about them was gradually stilled.

Shortly after we got back to London, I noticed a magnificent model of a foxhound adorning Poirot's mantelpiece. In answer to my inquiring glance, Poirot nodded.

"*Mais oui*! I got my five hundred francs! Is he not a splendid fellow? I call him Giraud!"

A few days later Jack Renauld came to see us with a resolute expression on his face.

"Monsieur Poirot, I've come to say good-bye. I'm sailing for South America almost immediately. My father had large interests over the continent, and I mean to start a new life out there."

"You go alone, Monsieur Jack?"

"My mother comes with me—and I shall keep Stonor on as my secretary. He likes out-of-the-way parts of the world."

"No one else goes with you?"

Jack flushed.

"You mean—?"

"A girl who loves you very dearly—who has been willing to lay down her life for you."

"How could I ask her?" muttered the boy. "After all that has happened, could I go to her and—Oh, what sort of a lame story could I tell?"

"*Les femmes*—they have a wonderful genius for manufacturing crutches for stories like that."

"Yes, but—I've been such a damned fool."

"So have all of us, one time and another," observed Poirot philosophically.

But Jack's face had hardened.

"There's something else. I'm my father's son. Would anyone marry me, knowing that?"

"You are your father's son, you say. Hastings here will tell you that I believe in heredity—"

"Well, then—"

"Wait. I know a woman, a woman of courage and endurance, capable of great love, of supreme self-sacrifice—"

The boy looked up. His eyes softened.

"My mother!"

"Yes. You are your mother's son as well as your father's. Then go to Mademoiselle Bella. Tell her everything. Keep nothing back—and see what she will say!"

Jack looked irresolute.

"Go to her as a boy no longer, but a man—a man bowed by the fate of the Past, and the fate of Today, but looking forward to a new and wonderful life. Ask her to share it with you. You may not realize it, but your love for each other has been tested in the fire and not found wanting. You have both been willing to lay down your lives for each other."

· · ·

And what of Captain Arthur Hastings, humble chronicler of these pages?

There is some talk of his joining the Renaulds on a ranch across the seas, but for the end of this story I prefer to go back to a morning in the garden of the Villa Geneviève.

"I can't call you Bella," I said, "since it isn't your name. And Dulcie seems so unfamiliar. So it's got to be Cinderella. Cinderella married the Prince, you remember. I'm not a Prince, but—"

She interrupted me.

"Cinderella warned him, I'm sure. You see, she couldn't promise to turn into a princess. She was only a little scullion after all—"

"It's the Prince's turn to interrupt," I interpolated. "Do you know what he said?"

"No?"

" 'Hell!' said the Prince—and kissed her!"

And I suited the action to the word.

About the Author

Agatha Christie is the most widely published author of all time and in any language, outsold only by the Bible and Shakespeare. Her books have sold more than a billion copies in English and another billion in a hundred foreign languages. She is the author of eighty crime novels and short-story collections, nineteen plays, two memoirs, and six novels written under the name Mary Westmacott.

She first tried her hand at detective fiction while working in a hospital dispensary during World War I, creating the now legendary Hercule Poirot with her debut novel *The Mysterious Affair at Styles*. With *The Murder at the Vicarage*, published in 1930, she introduced another beloved sleuth, Miss Jane Marple. Additional series characters include the husband-and-wife crime-fighting team of Tommy and Tuppence Beresford, private investigator Parker Pyne, and Scotland Yard detectives Superintendent Battle and Inspector Japp.

Many of Christie's novels and short stories were adapted into plays, films, and television series. *The Mousetrap*, her most famous play of all, opened in 1952 and is the longest-running play in history. Among her best-known film adaptations are *Murder on the Orient Express* (1974) and *Death on the Nile* (1978), with Albert Finney and Peter

Ustinov playing Hercule Poirot, respectively. On the small screen Poirot has been most memorably portrayed by David Suchet, and Miss Marple by Joan Hickson and subsequently Geraldine McEwan and Julia McKenzie.

Christie was first married to Archibald Christie and then to archaeologist Sir Max Mallowan, whom she accompanied on expeditions to countries that would also serve as the settings for many of her novels. In 1971 she achieved one of Britain's highest honors when she was made a Dame of the British Empire. She died in 1976 at the age of eighty-five. Her one hundred and twentieth anniversary was celebrated around the world in 2010.

www.AgathaChristie.com

Center Point Large Print
600 Brooks Road / PO Box 1
Thorndike ME 04986-0001 USA

(207) 568-3717

US & Canada:
1 800 929-9108
www.centerpointlargeprint.com